The Duke of Ruin

DEDICATION

For my Dad, for all your support down the years —and for never once gambling away my hand in marriage!

CONTENTS

London had been sweltering under an unforgivable heatwave since the middle of May. In elegantly appointed ballrooms across the capital women stood perspiring delicately, whilst cooling themselves with folding fans, which had undergone a sudden resurgence in popularity. The menfolk fared less well, as fans were a female contraption, and red-faced males were seen everywhere, sweating profusely and cursing the close humidity of the city. The Season was ratcheting up to be a disaster, young debutantes swooned, suffocating on the overwhelming stench of body odour that tainted each event, and older matrons, flushed and uncomfortable, declared their intent to return to the countryside as soon as was socially permissible.

Parliament adjourned the day after Ascot, and the ton breathed a sigh of relief: they could return home to swelter in private. As the servants began to pack up the town houses of their aristocratic owners, to everyone's surprise Lady Jersey declared she would be hosting one final ball before town emptied completely. This announcement was met outwardly with feigned enthusiasm; whilst most of the ton wished to leave the Capital post haste, Lady Jersey was not someone that one could simply just snub. And so, on the first night of June, hundreds of London's most fashionable families reluctantly descended on St. James' Square for one last hurrah.

Among their numbers was Miss Olive Greene, who at three and twenty was making a rather late debut into society. Everyone was in agreement that the flame-haired young woman was a beauty, and that it was a pity that she hadn't come out much sooner. An even greater pity, it was agreed, was that Olive had no dowry to speak of, though given her father's distasteful behaviour at the gaming tables, this was no shock. Olive herself cared little for what people had to say about her, kind or otherwise. Having spent the duration of her younger years dreaming of how magnificent a season in London would be, she found the reality rather disappointing. This was, perhaps, because she had changed so much from the naive, vain and lazy girl she had been, to a young woman who, after her mother's death, had transformed into a mature, practical and hardworking lady.

Her transformation was mostly on account of her father's gambling, which had spiralled out of control since Lady Greene's death. Olive had become the skivvy, cook and footman when the servants had been let go because they could no longer pay them, as well as an amateur accountant and keen negotiator with the many bailiffs who called to Rose Cottage, the family seat in Frome.

The February just gone however, her father had won a large sum in his club in Bristol, and had immediately written to his sister, outlining his plans for Olive to finally have a season. He would not listen to Olive's reasoning that the money would be better spent on the house, or saved for a rainy day, and instead she found herself shipped off to London, with a trunk full of new dresses that would be worthless in a few months' time.

Her Aunt had launched two daughters successfully, who were now happily married to the younger son of an Earl and an untitled but wealthy industrialist respectively, but she found Olive far less biddable than her teenage daughters had been.

"Don't glare so much Olive," Aunt Thea had admonished, after a disastrous night at Almack's Assembly Rooms. "The way you look at men makes them think that they are challenging you to a dawn duel, not asking you to dance."

Olive tried and failed, to feel some sort of contrition at her Aunt's words, but she was too worldly now to find excitement in a bloated, whiskey-nosed, son of the ton asking her to mark her dance card with his name. The young bloods held little allure, for in each of them she could see the same self-destructive, indulgent streaks that tainted her own father's soul. Alcohol and gambling were the stalwart occupations of men with too much money and time on their hands, and their profligate ways disgusted her. They, in turn, recognised that she was not like the other white-dressed, debutantes, who smiled submissively at them and dared not speak above a whisper. There was a restless energy about Olive that made the men uncomfortable. They wanted passive, compliant wives, not a woman with spirit; spirit was what one looked for in a horse.

"Lady Cowper remarked that you looked pained at her musicale," Aunt Thea chided after another disastrous outing, "She said you wore the look of a man being sent to the stockades."

That's because I don't belong here, Olive thought glumly. She no longer fit into the world of high society, a world that she had been schooled for since birth. The strict rules of decorum were suffocating her, and she did not know how to subdue her stubbornness and behave like a proper lady. She did not know how to be meek, innocent or naive, and she viewed the other women looking for husbands as being like beautiful birds, seeking to flit from one gold cage to another. Did they not understand that they were putting their lives at the mercy of young, reckless men, who did not know the value of anything?

And so, on that humid evening in June, Olive found herself playing the wallflower in a quiet alcove in Lady Jersey's ballroom. Not out of shyness, but rather, because, she wanted to commit to memory the glamour and the glitz of her surroundings. For she knew, with her father's worsening luck and her own stubborn refusal to entertain any young men, that this would be the last London ball she would attend. Tonight's extravaganza would instead serve as fodder for future daydreams, which would gloss over the fact that the men were not princes but toads on their way to a bad case of gout. For Olive, practical though she was, loved to daydream, a habit inflamed by the Gothic novels she devoured. At night she imagined finding love with a pirate, or a soldier - men who knew how to be men - who challenged her, and treated her as an equal. It was all rather scandalous, and she shared these thoughts with no one but her pillow.

As Olive gazed dreamily at the couples dancing the last dance of the night—a waltz— she sensed she was being watched, the hairs on the back of her neck stood up, and she shivered at the queer sensation. She turned slightly, to find a tall, brooding gentleman staring at her, with a dark, unreadable expression. He was large, much larger, than most; his hair dark and his skin tan, where other men were pasty pale. He was leaning casually against a marble column, seemingly uncaring that his avid, singular attention to her was quite scandalous, should it be noted by anyone wishing to be scandalized. Olive's green eyes met his blue, with what was meant to be an admonishing glare, but the intimidating boor seemed to take it as a sign to approach her.

"What's a pretty little thing like you, doing hiding away in a corner?" the stranger growled softly, like a bear, as he reached her side.

Olive shivered at his words, though the night was humid, and the ballroom unbearably hot from the crush of bodies that filled it. This was not the opening gambit of a proper gentleman.

"Avoiding wholly unsuitable men, such as yourself," she replied with a bravado she did not quite feel, for the dark stranger was most unnerving.

Two thick black eyebrows raised in appreciation of her candour; she would not play fashionably demure and frail simply because she was intimidated.

"My, my," the stranger laughed, though the mellow sound of mirth did not meet his eyes. "You have quite a tongue on you. Why have we not met before now, I wonder?"

"This is my first season out, sir." Olive replied shortly, before turning away from him to watch the dancers. Not that she was interested in them anymore, it was just that his penetrating gaze felt almost like he was undressing her. Heat quenched her cheeks, and she knew that the porcelain skin of her neck and décolletage had turned an awful shade of tomato. Such was the trial of having auburn hair; ones' feelings were on display for the world to witness.

"Aren't you a bit long in the tooth to be a debutant?" the stranger snorted, most rudely.

"And aren't you too far past thirty to be behaving like a school boy?" she countered, gathering her skirts, and making to leave.

A strong, tanned hand reached out and encircled her wrist, preventing her from moving.

"Allow me to apologize," the man's face wore a closed, guarded look, though his eyes were searching hers, as though he were trying to read her very thoughts. "I am Everleigh."

Everleigh; The Duke of Ruin. The man who was rumoured to have murdered his wife, and killed her lover in a duel. Liv must have visibly blanched, for the Duke quirked an amused eyebrow.

"Do I frighten you?" he asked, the corners of his sensuous mouth lifting up into a cruel leer. He seemed to find her fear terribly amusing.

"Not one jot," Olive shrugged; she had faced down bailiffs, and ruffians on her father's behalf- a rake of a Duke could not scare her. "I doubt that even you would be so bold as to murder me in a ball room, your Grace."

Olive relished the look of surprise on the Duke's handsome face as he digested her audacious remark, she supposed that no-one ever outwardly acknowledged the rumours which swirled around him. But then, what did she care if she upset the pompous prig? She would not have another season, the threat of being refused an Almack's voucher held little weight. Though she doubted that the Duke of Everleigh would find a warm welcome there either; his presence amongst the ton was only barely tolerated. His money and power outweighed his many misdeeds, but only just.

"Touché," Everleigh's lips quirked again. "I can see I underestimated you Miss –"

"Greene," Olive reluctantly supplied, for she had not wished to share her name with him. "Olive Greene."

"What an unfortunate name," Everleigh laughed properly this time, and he was even more handsome because of it. His colouring was dark, but his eyes were blue, and when he laughed they were as warm and bright as sunlight sparkling on the sea. The Duke's hand still circled Olive's wrist, and she tugged it lightly, wishing to free herself. He was dangerous, she knew it inherently. He was the embodiment of all her fantasies: dark, handsome, deadly. Olive was struck by the sudden realisation that one's fantasies were safer when they confined themselves to one's head and did not appear miraculously embodied in a ballroom. Nothing had ever scared her as much as the Duke of Everleigh, and it was not the man himself that petrified her, but her reaction. She wanted to flee, but worse, she wanted him to chase her. Her heart beat rapidly in her chest, and she had to steel herself before she spoke again.

"I am well aware of how silly my name is, your Grace," she responded through gritted teeth. "And, unlike you, I am also well aware of what constitutes a scandalous amount of time for a man and woman to spend conversing alone in an alcove. We have exceeded it ten-fold. Good night, your Grace."

At last, Olive had managed to yank her wrist free from his strong grip, and she made to push past him, to find her Aunt.

"Don't go, just yet," the Duke blocked her path with his body, an act which was akin to rolling a boulder in her way, he was that large and immovable. "I wish to apologise for upsetting you."

"I don't wish to hear your apology," Olive whispered, slightly breathless from a heady mixture of fear and desire. "An apology requires actual remorse, and I doubt you are capable of that."

"You seem to have the measure of me already."

Instead of being insulted, Everleigh looked rather pleased. He watched her as a cat might watch a mouse, amused by her antics, but she knew she was only safe so long as he found her entertaining.

"That's nothing to be proud of, your Grace," Olive whispered, her face now flushed with anger. "I should hate for anyone to think that of me."

"Then that's where you and I differ, Miss Greene," the Duke inclined his head. "I care little for other people's opinions."

He stepped out of her way, and waved his arm, indicating that he would allow her to pass. Olive lifted her skirts, but when she made to walk past him, he again blocked her way.

"I have enjoyed our chat immensely, Miss Greene," he whispered in a way that was almost a threat, "And rest assured, we shall meet again."

With a smirk, he was gone, leaving Olive standing stupefied by the marble column. She did not know what it was about her that had attracted the Duke's attention, but she wished dearly that she hadn't.

A season to find a husband, and the only man I attract has a penchant for murder, she thought wryly to herself. She had her father's luck.

A fine mist of rain lashed down on the Sixth Duke of Everleigh as he made his way on horseback, up the steep incline of White Ladies Road. The grand, yellow-stone buildings, which lined either side of his path, were as beautiful as those found in the neighbouring city of Bath. The stones here, however, were blemished from smoke and coal soot, for Bristol, unlike its sedate, fashionable neighbour, was a city built on industry, and it was stained with grime to its very core.

Which suited Ruan Winston Charles Ashford just fine, for he too was neither sedate nor fashionable, and there were many that would say he was stained to the core; that his very soul was black from his all misdeeds. There were many more again, he thought with a rueful grin, who would say that this was balderdash, that he had no soul to stain. Not that Ruan gave a tuppence for what people said of him, or the rumours that were whispered in parlour rooms and gentleman's clubs across the whole of England.

He had killed a man.

He had murdered his wife.

He was the Duke of Ruin.

The last rumour was the only one that the Duke would allude to publicly, for it was partly true. He rarely gambled, but when he did, he played for high stakes. And he always won. Many a young blood had lost more than his shirt to the Duke.

"A fool and his money, are easily parted," Ruan would quip, when asked if he felt any qualms at all about blighting the futures of these entitled, young Lords. They had ruined their own lives, he reasoned; he had just profited from it.

The genteel, moneyed, borough of Clifton, which looked out over the Avon Gorge from its lofty perch atop the hills of the city, was quiet, for the hour was late. Ruan dismounted his stallion, and handed the reins, without a word, to the doorman of the club. The poor chap was soaked, and he looked grateful to have an excuse to seek respite from the weather, even if only momentarily. The interior bar of the club was empty when he entered it, but from the adjoining snug room came the sound that Ruan loved the most. The sound of money exchanging hands.

"Gentlemen," he said brusquely, removing his hat, which was sodden from the miserable weather. He ran a hand through his thick black hair, to remove the worst of the raindrops, and surveyed the players present; the usual mix of wealthy merchants and country squires. The elite of the ton would never deign to grace a place like this, preferring the Assembly Rooms in Bath, which was precisely why Ruan was there. He had no patience for gout ridden Viscounts or elderly Earls, and definitely no time for their wives and daughters, who could not keep the fear-tinged fascination from their faces when they met him. Murderer, he could see them think when their eyes met his, before they quickly looked away.

"Mascotte," Ruan said with a nod as he took a seat at the gaming table next to a portly man of about fifty years. Gregg Mascotte was England's most notorious gossip, a skill he put to good use as editor the Bristol Daily Star. No doubt the rag would be filled with veiled hints of his escapades the next day, for though the public loathed him, they loved to read of his adventures.

"Your Grace," Mascotte's florid, puffy face broke in to a grin. "You're playing?"

"I am," Ruan conceded.

"Then I must count myself out," Mascotte raised his hands in defeat, giving an ingratiating laugh. "I know when I'm in over my head."

"If only other men were as wise, sir," Ruan murmured as he waited to be dealt in.

The other unwise men who remained at the table were familiar to him; bankers, merchants and industrialists who had money enough to fritter away. The only man that Ruan was not acquainted with, was Lord Greene, who held an impoverished baronetcy in nearby Frome. He was legendary for having won and lost his fortune at least several times over the six decades of his life, though rumour now had it, that, since his wife's death, Lord Greene had been losing more than winning of late. Ruan hid a smile, he intended to see Lord Greene ruined that night, for the man had something he desired very much: his daughter's hand. The defiant emerald eyes, of Miss Greene, had haunted his dreams for the past two weeks. Ruan was not a man who believed in love at first sight, though he did recognise lust when it reared its hungry head. Olive Greene had stirred him in a way that no woman had been able to for quite some time. He was a jaded, connoisseur of women, both titled ladies and some of common birth, but Miss Greene had captivated his mind - and other parts of his body - most thoroughly with her luscious beauty, and sharp tongue. He liked a woman with spirit, though they were hard to find amongst the ton, who tended to breed insipid dishcloths as daughters. Now that he had found a woman who might challenge him, Ruan intended to make her his wife, for the need to produce an heir was foremost on his mind, and the thoughts of producing one with Olive was most titillating indeed.

"What's the buy in?" he asked, as the cards were dealt.

"Ten pounds, your Grace," William Cheevers, who owned Bristol's largest shipping company, supplied helpfully through teeth which were clenching a cheroot.

"Let's see if we can't make this a bit more interesting," Ruan drawled, quirking his eyebrow sardonically. Ten pounds was a pittance in his eyes, barely worth shuffling a deck for.

The Duke of Everleigh removed his jacket, and loosened his cravat before summoning a footman to fetch him a brandy; if things went to plan, this would be a long night and he might as well get comfortable. He cut a dashing figure at the table, especially when compared to the other men. Where they were puffed and middle aged, he was young and fit. He had the body of an athlete; broad, muscular shoulders, which tapered into a narrow waist and an enviable flat stomach. His hair was jet black, and his ice blue eyes contrasted with the tan skin of his face. The Duke, unlike his pale companions, spent most of his time outdoors, and it showed.

The group played hard and fast at five card loo. The buy-in was raised several times to astronomical sums, and soon the five players had been reduced to but two: The Duke of Everleigh and Lord Greene —just as he had planned.

"I think you've been well and truly looed, my Lord," Ruan said with a satisfied smile as he revealed his own cards to be a flush. Four of the same suit and the coveted Pam, laid out on the table for all to see.

Lord Greene's face fell when he saw that he had lost again. In the last round he had staked his country pile to the pool, and as the winner of each trick, Everleigh could now add a stately home in Frome to his list of properties. Not that he would even notice it, he had that many estates dotted about the British Isles.

"Oh, God," Greene dropped his head into his hands, his face ghoulishly pale. Ruan surveyed his bald pate unsympathetically; the man had failed to win anything for the last few games, but instead of decreasing his bets, or passing all together, Greene had insisted on raising the stakes. A bad move, if one was to judge by his current expression of despair.

"I'll tell you what," Ruan said softly, his blue eyes narrowed thoughtfully, looking for all the world as though an idea had struck him, just at that moment. "How about another game, old man? I'll make it worth your while."

Lord Greene looked up, his face hopeful, whilst the gentlemen around the table shifted uncomfortably in their chairs. They had heard the Duke offer hope before, only to snatch it away cruelly; broken men with nothing to lose could be goaded into gambling even more. The only person who didn't look faintly perturbed was Mascotte, who had, until now, watched the game with a detached disinterest. Ruan could see the rotund editor wrestling with a sly smile at the thought that he might see Lord Greene humiliated even further. Humiliation sold papers aplenty.

"Do you wish to cut another deck, your Grace?" Lord Greene asked, with no little confusion. The poor sod had nothing left to gamble with, for the Duke now owned it all; he could not play for another trick.

"No more loo," Ruan waved a dismissive hand at the idea. "And no other players. Just you and I, Lord Greene. Lets make it a game of hazard."

"What are the stakes?" the elderly Baron asked dumbly. "For I've nothing left to play with, unless you want the old nag I rode in on."

Macotte snorted, and even the other men at the table gave a laugh, though they were silenced by a dark look from Ruan.

"You have one thing I want," he said lightly, holding the old man's gaze. "Your daughter."

Silence filled the room, bar the laboured breathing of the Daily Star's editor, who seemed fit to explode with excitement at the turn of events.

"Olive?" Lord Greene sounded out his daughter's name slowly, as though it was unfamiliar to him. Judging by the amount of time he spent in clubs and gaming hells, Ruan reasoned that it probably was. It was a wonder the man could even remember he had a daughter, let alone her name.

"The very one," Ruan smiled. "If you win, everything you have lost will be restored to you. But If I win, then Olive's hand in marriage is mine, and mine alone."

Lord Greene raised his eyebrows appreciatively at the generous offer, though his expression remained worried.

"A daughter's hand is not something a man should gamble with," he said, tugging at the collar of his shirt. He sounded as though he were trying to remind himself of that fact, rather than believing it fully.

"Most women dream of becoming a Duchess," Ruan countered, though he could see the other's collectively thinking: Not your Duchess.

For, as the rumour went, Ruan had killed his last wife. It was half true, and because of it, he was the last man that any loving father would want his daughter to wed. Duke or no Duke.

"I don't know," Lord Greene looked wistfully at the table. He was tempted, or half tempted at least. Ruan sighed with annoyance, he would have to sweeten his offer.

"If you lose," he said evenly, drumming his fingers on the table impatiently. "I shall have Olive's hand, but I will also restore your estates to you as goodwill gesture. A marriage gift of sorts."

Each man at the table metaphorically scratched their heads at the conundrum now facing Lord Greene. If he staked his daughters hand, no matter what the outcome of the game, he would surely see his fortunes restored. But what kind of man would gamble with his own daughter as the stakes?

"And if you lose, your Grace?" Lord Greene sounded braver, though his hands trembled.

"That does not matter, my Lord, I never do."

Ruan smiled and the men surrounding him chuckled.

Buoyed by the thought of placing a bet he could only stand to gain from, Lord Greene quickly agreed to the terms, and two dice were fetched. Ruan allowed the older man to cast the first die, and it soon became apparent that Lord Greene had as much skill at Hazard as he had at five card loo.

In each of his rounds the older man rolled successive twos and threes, his face becoming paler and his hand shakier with each throw.

"Well," Mascotte said gleefully, as the Duke won four out of five of his own throw ins. "It seems I shall be the first to congratulate you on your upcoming nuptials, your Grace."

"Shall we play for the best out of three games?" Lord Greene stuttered, as he realised that he had lost. His grey face showed signs of dawning comprehension at what he had done, and none of the men present seemed able to look him in the eye.

"No," Ruan shook his head firmly, ignoring the old man's nervous protests. "We shall play no more games, my Lord. I shall meet you at your home tomorrow at noon. Instruct your daughter to be ready."

"But the banns," Lord Greene grasped at straws. "You cannot wed until the banns are read out – that takes three weeks at least. Unless you wait a day or two for a special license."

"There's no need."

Ruan reached for his coat on the back of the chair, and from its inside pocket he withdrew the papers of the special license, which the Archbishop of Canterbury had signed for him just that very morning.

"You already had it?" Lord Greene looked flabbergasted, his mouth opening and closing like a fish out of water. "So, all along...?"

"All along, I only wanted your daughter's hand," Ruan conceded, with a smile that did not reach his cold blue eyes. "And now I have it. My thanks, Lord Greene. I shall see you anon."

Ruan swept from the room, not caring to look over his shoulder, where he was sure a broken Lord Greene would be seeking comfort and solace from his friends. He would not get it.

Even Ruan, cold hearted swine that he was, would not have gambled away his daughter's life to a man with a reputation for murdering his last spouse, among other misdeeds. Lord Greene had thought he could not lose, how wrong he had been. The despicable act would surly eat at the old bugger for the rest of his years. Another life ruined – though the Duke thought it most deserved in this case. Imagine having a daughter as beautiful as the unfortunately named Miss Olive Greene, and throwing away her hand on a game of chance. It beggared belief.

He was already looking forward to the next morning, when he would make Olive his Duchess, and parts of him stirred at the thought of making her completely his. T'was a pity the young woman clearly hadn't felt the same way about him, but the Duke was sure she would learn to tolerate him after a lifetime of marriage.

Ruan smiled broadly at the doorman, as he handed him the reins to his stallion.

"Did you have a good night, your Grace?" the footman inquired, taken aback by how jovial the usually dour Duke of Everleigh appeared.

"It was," Ruan laughed, "For me at least."

Olive was in the kitchen, kneading bread into what she hoped would be an edible loaf, when her father emerged the next morning. His presence filled the room with the stale scent of cheroot smoke and the distinct odour of brandy. Olive sniffed; copious amounts of brandy, it would seem.

"What did you lose last night?" she asked bitterly, taking the misshapen lump of dough, and placing it on a tray. "The tapestries? The candlesticks? You're still wearing your shirt, so you didn't lose that at least."

"Liv," her father's voice was raspy, and she could hear the phlegm on his chest from the heavy smoking the night before. "A cup of tea would be nice, before you begin your inquisition."

"There's a pot on the table."

Liv watched from the corner of her eye as her father made his way to the wooden table, which dominated the other side of the dark, spotlessly clean kitchen. Only three years ago, before her mother's untimely demise, there would have been servants to make her father his morning brew, and it would have been served to him in the dining room. But now there were no servants, there wasn't even a table in the echoing dining room – it had been sold, along with the paintings and a heap of other furniture, to pay her father's ever accruing debts.

Irritated, Liv placed the baking tray in the wood burning oven, and slammed the door. She did not mind hard work, in fact she preferred it to the more tedious feminine arts like needle point and flower pressing. What she minded, as anyone would, was the uncertainty that all her hard work would be for nothing.

Her father had been a profligate gambler before her mother's death, but since then had become wild and reckless with his gaming. Some mornings Liv woke not knowing if the bed she had slept in would still be there that night, or if the roof above her head would have to be sold.

"Here," she snapped, ladling out two soft boiled eggs into egg cups and placing them before her father. A slice of dry, two-day old bread accompanied them, which her father looked at askance.

"I had to walk to the far field this morning, to collect the eggs, for that's where the stupid hen decided to nest," she said by way of explanation, "I had no time to make you fresh bread."

"Never mind," her father sighed, picking up a knife and generously coating the offending bread with a thick coating of butter. "I have news for you Liv, great news."

Liv stilled; the last time her father had given her great news, was after he had won thousands of pounds at the tables. Enough to send her to London, for her first season and look at what a disaster that had turned out to be. In hind-sight, Liv now wished that she had just hidden the money as a nest egg for herself, instead of allowing him to convince her to fritter it away on dresses and baubles. She had returned to Frome deflated, and just as penniless and trapped as she had left it.

"What kind of great news, Papa?" she asked cautiously, taking a seat across from her father, who looked rather green around the gills. A big win, if she could manage to wrestle some money from him, might mean they could hire a girl to help around the house. She might even be able to refurnish some of the main rooms, so that she could invite some of the few friends she had made in London to stay.

"A husband," her father said, gravely setting his cup upon the table. "I have found you a husband, my dear."

Olive, for the first time in her life, felt as though she was going to faint. A feeling she quickly dismissed; only consumptives and elderly matrons fainted, and she was neither.

"And who is this man you've gambled me away to?" she asked, her voice laden with ice, for she intuitively knew just how her father had found her a husband. "A farmer? A criminal? The captain of a pirate ship?"

Each was a distinct possibility, for her father's sense of reason and decency left him completely when he gambled.

"None of those," Lord Greene said, waving a dismissive hand, as though Liv's concerns were irrelevant. "I have promised you to England's most eligible bachelor: The Duke of Everleigh."

Oh goodness, no.

Liv felt the acrid taste of bile, rising in her throat; anyone but him. The Duke of Everleigh had haunted her dreams since their meeting at Lady Jersey's. Olive, under the guise of paying a social call, had extracted from her neighbour, the elderly Lady Engleman, who lived in nearby Blatchbridge, exactly what had happened with the Duke's previous wife. Her name had been Catherine Keyford, the daughter of the Cornish Lord Keyford and she had been two and twenty years of age when Everleigh had married her and made her a Duchess.

"She'd never even had a season," Lady Engleman had whispered, sharing the scandal as she poured Liv a cup of tea. "Is it any wonder the girl behaved as she did?"

"Oh?" Liv had sipped her tea innocently, hoping that Lady Engleman would continue with her tale.

"She took a lover," the old matron whispered, though because of her hearing the whisper was delivered at the same level as a shout. The young maid who hovered by the door, began to giggle, but quickly stopped at Liv's glare. Not that she blamed the girl for laughing, but she did not want Lady Engleman's attention diverted by scolding a servant.

"She told Everleigh that she was leaving him for this chap, and the Duke called the young man out," Lady Engleman had continued, oblivious to the fact that both Olive and the maid were hanging on her every word. "He shot him dead, with one bullet between the eyes, or so the story goes. And then he returned to his estate in Cornwall, and the next thing we heard the poor Duchess was dead."

"How?" Liv gasped, wondering how the callow Everleigh had disposed of his wife. Was it in a fit of passionate rage? Or did he plan it coolly and meticulously?

"The official word was that she fell down the stairs," the older woman coughed discreetly, to indicate that she hadn't bought into that story. "But everyone knew it was him. His own mother ran off on her marriage to his father, when he was but a boy. To have his wife attempt to do the same must have driven him insane with rage."

Liv sipped her tea again, as she digested this tit-bit of gossip. She couldn't picture the Duke as a young boy, and felt no sympathy for him whatsoever. Plenty of people's mothers abandoned them, it didn't give them carte blanche to murder their wives! She had left Lady Engleman's feeling faintly perturbed that she had exchanged any words with the villainous Duke, and now, this very morning she found she was betrothed to him!

"Oh goodness, Papa," she groaned, allowing her head to fall into her hands in despair. "What have you done? Do you not know what they said he did to his last wife?"

"All balderdash," Lord Greene waved her concerns away with his hand, as though brushing away a bothersome fly, though he did look rather uncomfortable that she had brought up the alleged murder. "He seemed most keen to make you his wife – he even had a special license written up in anticipation that I would consent."

"Consent?"

A laugh so bitter it shocked the pair of them, ripped from Liv's throat. "You consented to nothing," she whispered, her hands gripping the edge of the table so hard that her knuckles turned white. "You gambled me away as surely as you gambled away the paintings, the horses, and the furniture— and I can never forgive you for that."

She pushed her chair away from the table, and stood up, running an agitated hand through her thick red curls.

"W-where are you going?" her father stuttered nervously, "He'll be here before noon."

"I am going to pay my last respects to my Mother," Liv replied, not looking him in the eye. "For when I leave this house today, you may rest assured that I will never return."

With that, Liv left the room, slamming the door behind her, so hard that it nearly came off its hinges.

A dirt path, surrounded on either side by wild hedgerows laden with summer blooms led to the small, squat church where her mother lay buried, not five minutes away. Liv passed by the headstones of many more deceased Greenes as she picked her way through the cemetery, for her father's family had been seated in Frome for centuries and her ancestors had all lived and died here.

"Oh mother," Liv sighed, as she reached the small, granite headstone which bore her mother's name. "I wish you were here."

Every day Liv wished that her mother was still alive, for Lila Greene had been a formidable woman and only person who had been able to rein in her father's wild impulses. If she was still here, Liv had no doubt, that this marriage to Everleigh would not be happening. She would be safe, perhaps married to a staid country solicitor, and not panicking at the thought that she had been sold to a Duke with a predication for murder.

"It seems I am between a rock and a hard place Mama," she whispered aloud, as she hunkered down to clear the few dandelions that had boldly grown since her last visit.

The very idea of marrying the Duke of Everleigh sent shivers down her spine; but the thought of remaining at the mercy of her father's gambling addiction was even worse.

What Liv longed for, more than anything, was freedom. She wanted to be the master of her own destiny, not some small, insignificant woman, at the mercy of men's whims and desires. With a final, fond pat of the grass, which was now free of weeds, she stood and squared her shoulders.

Life had seemed intent of late, of throwing chaos and destruction her way, and Liv had quickly come to realise that the only way to survive, was to face that chaos head on.

She would master the disreputable Duke, she thought grimly, she would tame this man who appeared to think her life an amusing plaything, and she would make him rue the day he decided he wanted to marry her.

"Good God, man, are you nervous?"

Henry Lavelle, Viscount Somerset glanced at his old friend the Duke of Everleigh with wonder. They were standing at the front door of Rosewick Cottage, Lord Greene's home, which in the usual English way was not a cottage at all, but rather an impressive Manor House. Three stories high, and built of soft, butter-yellow Bath stone, it was a rather impressive old pile.

Ruan momentarily rued his decision to gift it back to the profligate gambler, for one day he would surely lose it again, but the deed was now done. As a man of honour – for the most part – he would not renege on a gentleman's agreement.

Though it appeared that the old reprobate Lord Greene might have decided to take back what he had promised him.

"Hello?" Ruan banged against the door with his fist once more, where was the footman or the butler? Had the whole house absconded with Miss Greene at the news of her impending nuptials?

"Hang on, hang on," the sound of a man's grumbling filtered out the wooden door, much to Viscount Somerset's amusement.

"You're early."

It was Lord Greene himself, dressed much as he had been the night before. Ruan gave a discreet sniff, and tried not to wince; from the smell of the old man it appeared he was still wearing last night's brandy soaked shirt.

"I'm not early," an aggrieved Ruan consulted his gold pocket watch, it had just struck noon. He was perfectly on time.

A silence ensued, in which a curious Lord Greene surveyed the well-dressed Viscount Somerset, who was flamboyantly garbed in a coat of plum. Despite his rather obstreperous taste in clothing, Lavelle was Ruan's closest friend. Only friend, if truth be told. They had grown up together as young men, their Cornwall estates sharing a common land border, and Lavelle was possibly the only person who could reconcile today's dark despised Duke of Everleigh with the innocent young lad he had once been.

"Lavelle," Ruan removed his hat, "Allow me to introduce Lord Greene. Lord Greene, this is Henry Lavelle, Viscount Somerset."

"How do you do," Lord Greene responded churlishly, his West-County accent sounding more pronounced than it had the night before.

"Do you want to come in?" he asked, his face clearly betraying the hope that Everleigh would miraculously say no to the invitation. He opened the door begrudgingly when they informed him that they did wish to enter his home, and ushered them inside with a scowl.

"Where is she?" Ruan asked, glancing around the bare front hall. It was bright, with a double-height ceiling, though the sunshine only highlighted how sparse the furnishings were. There were noticeably large, dark square patches of wallpaper dotted throughout the room. Places where pictures had once hung, Ruan guessed, pictures which had probably been sold to pay Lord Greene's gaming debts.

Which reminded him of the prize he was there to collect.

"Where is your daughter?"

"I'm here," an irritated voice called down from above their heads.

Ruan looked up, and saw Olive standing on the stairs with one hand on the mahogany banister, while her other hand held a battered portmanteau. She was breath-taking, her red curls pinned high on her head, her green eyes narrowed in displeasure at the sight of him, and her body – Ruan's mouth went dry – was clad in a simple red gown, which clung to her generous bosom, before falling elegantly to the floor.

"Allow me to assist you with your bags," he said, realising that he had been seizing her up like she was a horse at Tattersalls, and not his intended wife.

"There's no need," Olive snapped, making her own way down the stairs and unceremoniously dumping her bag on the ground. It landed with a bang, which echoed in the empty hallway.

"May I introduce Lord Lavelle?" Ruan ignored the mutinous look his bride to be had cast him. She was a feisty one, he thought with a smile, which was exactly what he wanted in a wife. Someone with a bit of spirit, to challenge him, and she would preferably do this challenging in the bedroom.

"I've had the great pleasure of meeting Miss Greene before." Lavelle took Olive's hand, and placed a perfunctory kiss on it, which left Ruan seething with an emotion he could not identify. When Olive flushed with pleasure at the Viscount's attentions, he soon realised what it was: jealousy. It roared in his chest like a lion, and for one stupid second, the Duke considered placing his body between his friend and his fiancé to separate them. How dare Lavelle presume he could touch her? And how dare Olive think that she could bestow her beautiful smile on anyone bar him?

Reason slowly descended, brought on by Lavelle's amused laugh, as he noted Ruan's displeasure.

"I wonder where the Vicar has got to?" the Viscount mused, ambling over to the open door, to peer out into the driveway. "For I fear a bloody massacre, if he doesn't show up soon."

Ruan grunted; he knew that he had been glaring at his friend, and he knew that when he glared he was most formidable indeed. He cast a sly glance at Olive, who had paled somewhat, but whose mouth remained in a resolute, firm line.

"I apologise," she said, after an uncomfortable pause, "For not having any refreshments, or even a luncheon to offer you gentlemen. News of the nuptials came as quite a surprise, and as such I had no time to prepare."

Lavelle guffawed at her peevish tone, casting Ruan a knowing glance.

"I'm afraid that when the Duke decides he wants something," Lavelle said impishly, "That he waits for neither time nor tide."

"That's not how the saying goes," Ruan interjected, wishing to add his voice to the conversation, if only so that Olive would bestow her gaze upon him and not his friend. He surveyed the look that passed between the Viscount and his betrothed with a frown; was she flirting with Lavelle, or simply conversing with him? The thought was driving him to distraction, and he wished to God that the Vicar would hurry up, so that he could whisk her away from the gaze of any other man but him.

"Am I late?"

The jovial voice that called through the door, was soon accompanied by the rotund figure of Frome's Vicar. His jowls quivered from the exertion of plodding up the drive, and he wiped the rivulets of sweat from his forehead with a handkerchief. The Vicar had obviously downgraded the seven deadly sins to six, if his girth was anything to go by.

"You're just in time," Lavelle answered smoothly, shaking the man's hand and ushering him inside. "Our groom was about to combust, but you'll soon see to that."

The Vicar chuckled good naturedly, and began to usher them into the drawing room.

"I've been told to make this quick," he said with a wink to Ruan, who scowled back in return. He had paid the man a handsome price to perform the ceremony at very short notice. A few babes would have their Christening pushed back to the afternoon as a result of his bribery, but so what? It wasn't as though an infant could tell the time, whereas he could, and he had never been a patient man.

"Let us begin," the Vicar said at last, when Olive and the Duke were standing side by side, before him in the drawing room.

The ceremony was very simple, with the couple exchanging their vows before their two witnesses; Lord Lavelle, who seemed to find the whole thing terribly amusing, and Lord Greene, who seemed fit to cast up his accounts on the carpet. Ruan looked down at his feet, under which there were only bare floorboards. There was no carpet to stain, Lord Greene having gambled it away.

"By the power invested in me," the Vicar boomed, after what seemed to Ruan to be an age, his face solemn, "I now pronounce you man and wife."

Olive flinched visibly at his words. Her face, already alabaster, was now a ghostly white. She looked almost ill at the pronouncement that she was now a Duchess.

Another wife less than enamoured with the thought of being married to me, Ruan thought wryly as he observed her reaction. At least this time he felt a flame of desire to the woman who had promised her life to him.

"What say you all to a drop of brandy, to toast the newlyweds?" the Vicar asked, rubbing his hands together with anticipation now that his part in the sorry affair was finished.

"No," Ruan replied shortly, reaching out to take Olive's hand in his own. He held it tightly, for fear that she may abscond. "My wife and I have a ship to catch."

The Vicar's mouth opened into an "O" of surprise, and the only thing which rescued the awkwardness of the moment was Lavelle.

"What Everleigh meant to say, Vicar," Lavelle flashed his winning smile at the man of the cloth, whilst elbowing his friend in the ribs. "Is that he regrets that he cannot accompany us to the pub, for a few celebratory sherries, but he has gifted me a coin purse to make sure that you, and the father of the bride, might toast the happy couple in their absence."

The Vicar looked mollified, and Lord Greene licked his parched lips. If ever a man had looked like he needed a pint, it was Lord Greene at that very moment. He seemed to have aged a decade over night, his shoulders were slumped and he wore a look of defeat on his lined face.

"Thank you, Lord Lavelle," Ruan nodded stiffly, he had never been good at the business of social niceties. He glanced at Olive before he spoke again, wishing to let her know that she was foremost in his thoughts; "I shall leave my wife to say her goodbye to her father."

"There's no need."

Olive Ashford, now Duchess of Everleigh, yanked her hand from his grip. "My bag is in the hallway," she said to her husband, in the tone one would use to address a footman. "If you would be so kind as to bring it to the carriage."

She turned and glanced at Lavelle and the Vicar.

"Good day gentlemen," she said, inclining her head. Her gaze did not fall in the direction of her father, who stared with an open mouth as his daughter swept from the room.

"Oh, dear," the Vicar said, tugging at his collar uncomfortably. "Whatever's going on here?"

"It's rather a long story," Ruan heard Lavelle say, but he didn't wait to hear the rest of his friend's explanations. He followed his angry wife from the room, remembering to retrieve her lone bag, and followed her out to the waiting carriage.

Olive sat with her arms folded across her chest, staring icily out the window, not even turning to acknowledge her husband as he took a seat opposite her.

"We are going to Bristol," he volunteered, as the carriage made its way through the winding streets of Frome. "After that we will board one of my ships and sail for Paris. How does that sound to you?"

"It sounds like I have no choice in the matter," Olive retorted, bestowing him, at last, with a glacial gaze. Good God, but she was beautiful when she was angry, Ruan thought, a surge of desire coursing through him.

"You don't," he conceded magnanimously, he could afford that now that she was his. "Have a choice. Though don't think that I shall be a tyrant for the whole of our marriage. Once you birth me a son, you will be free to do as you please. And well compensated, of course."

"Oh, of course," Olive mimicked his imperious tone, with alarming accuracy. "I suppose if I don't deliver this son in the required time, I will be disposed of like your last wife?"

Anger flowed through Ruan's veins at the accusation. He had heard it before, but coming from her it stung sharply.

"I did not kill my last wife," he said through gritted teeth.

"I'm sure that's what you say to everyone," Olive bit, apparently nonplussed by the smouldering Duke seated opposite her.

"Actually, no." Ruan replied, struggling to keep his tone even, and trying not to lose his temper, which when unleashed had a mind of its own. "I don't care who thinks I killed Catherine, but I will not have you thinking that I did. You are safe with me, you have my word."

The weight of his word seemed to have little impression on Olive, for she returned her gaze to the country road, which whisked by the window of the carriage.

"Why me?" she asked, after a lengthy silence, in which Ruan had wondered if perhaps he had been a bit too impatient with his plans. Actually asking the girl if she wished to be his wife, might have ingratiated him a little better with her.

"You are the most beautiful woman I have ever seen," he said simply, unembarrassed by his confession. "The moment I saw you, I knew that I had to have you as my own. I desire to continue on my line, and when I do, I'd rather do it with a beautiful woman like you, rather than some insipid Miss with a dowry I don't need."

To his pleasure, a pink flush began to form on his wife's cheeks, making its way down her neck to her décolletage, and the impressive swell of her breasts. Ruan lifted his gaze from her bosom, to her eyes, which were watching him with irritated amusement.

"Most men would try to court a woman they desired as a wife," she challenged him, her eyes narrow and thoughtful. "They would write love notes, and fill her dance card. They wouldn't try to win her in a game of chance."

"I am not most men," Ruan shrugged, thinking that the courtship rituals she had listed sounded insipid and dull.

"And I am not a piece of horseflesh to be bartered with."

The last sentence was spit with such venom, that Ruan recoiled slightly. He had made many women angry over the years, in fact it was one of the things he did best, but this woman, his wife, was so furious that Ruan believed if she had been in possession of a pistol, she would have shoot him there and then.

It was alarmingly alluring.

"You are not a piece of horseflesh," he agreed, hoping to placate her anger. "You are my wife, and anything that you desire shall be yours. Don't tell me that the life that I can offer you is less certain than living at the mercy of your profligate father?"

"I believe the expression, your Grace," Olive replied, in bored tones, unimpressed by his declaration. "Is caught between the devil and the deep, blue sea."

Ruan smiled with appreciation, for it was a sailor's expression. She thought him the devil, but as a man who had spent a decade of his life on the ocean, he knew that she could not fathom the dangers of dark, endless seas. Better she was under his care, the known devil, than at the mercy of her father. Who knew who, or what type of man, might have eventually won her hand. The thought left him shaken, which perplexed him. He was not inclined toward feelings of empathy or protectiveness, but his new wife seemed to be eliciting both.

"You may call me Ruan," was all he managed to say in response, his thoughts being occupied elsewhere.

"What kind of a name is that?" she asked, watching him with sloe eyes.

"Scottish," he thought briefly of his wild mother, who had bestowed on him a Highlander's name, before disappearing to the continent with one of his father's footmen. His last memory of her was when she had tucked him in to bed the night that she had left. She had smoothed his hair, and told him that she loved him, then left his life forever. Looking back now, he recognised that his mother had only been a child herself; though the memory of her leaving still seared through his soul.

The carriage carried on moving at a brusque pace, and soon they had passed Bath and were on the road to Bristol proper.

"Have you ever been to France?" he asked, to break the silence that had fallen between them again. With Catherine, their short marriage had been filled with silence and the pressure of things unsaid; Ruan wanted this to be different. He wanted Olive to feel free to speak to him.

"No," she answered shortly, tearing her eyes away from the window and glancing at him with disdain. "Do you think a father with a predication for gambling would ever have had the money to take me to Paris? When he lost we barely had money for food."

"Of course, I apologise," Ruan frowned; now that he thought on it, Paris had probably always been beyond her grasp. "You'll like it, I promise. You can have anything your heart desires. Now that you are my Duchess, you shall not want for a thing."

Olive looked at him, with the steady gaze that women the world over had mastered, reserved specifically for the times a man dared declare that he could give her anything her heart wished for.

 What do you know of my heart? He could see her thinking, and for the first time in his two and thirty years, he cursed the fact that he was born a male. Oh, to have the innate wisdom that women possessed, to feel as deeply as they did. He was a lumbering boar of a man, he knew that, and his desires were simple, not multi-layered and unobtainable - as he was sure Olive's, like every other woman's - were.

"Thank you, your Grace," his wife replied simply, her tone decidedly calm, dare he say, polite. She resumed her watch on the passing fields, leaving Ruan feeling bereft as her attention fell elsewhere.

He had no idea what it was that Olive wanted, but at that moment he would have killed to get it for her, a thought that scared him no end.

The port of Bristol was a hive of activity, dozens of tall ships were docked in their berths, and hundreds of sailors and tars milled around the cobblestoned pier, all watched over by the towering spires of St. Mary Radcliffe. Liv watched from the window of the carriage as labourers unloaded cargo from their vessels, whilst urchin children ran underfoot, seeking to collect anything that was dropped in the process.

"We're here," the Duke said, pointlessly Liv felt, for she had eyes in her head and she could see that they had arrived.

"Have you ever sailed before?" he asked again, waiting for a response. Her husband had a remarkably thick skull, Liv thought with a scowl, for patently she did not wish to speak with him, and yet he kept directing questions her way.

"I spent my childhood summers with my mother's family, on the coast of Devon," she offered, struggling to keep her face blank as memories of those glorious, hot days when she was safe and loved, resurfaced. "I have sailed in small boats, your Grace, and I am a capable swimmer, but I have never been aboard a ship."

"Ruan," he frowned at her, his gaze dark and forbidding, "I told you to call me Ruan."

"You did."

His face was awash with annoyance, apparently the Duke expected her to feel an innate familiarity with him now that they were married. Which was preposterous, because at her count, she had known him all of five hours. Soon she would know him in the Biblical sense, she thought with a slight jolt of fear. She knew little of what went on in the marital bedroom but, she glanced at the Duke from the corner of her eyes, she automatically knew that he would not be a dispassionate lover. She felt her face begin to flush at the wanton thoughts that stole over her, and was grateful when the liveried footman opened the door of the carriage for the newlyweds.

"The captain is here to meet you, your Grace," the handsome young man said, with a bow of deference to the Duke.

Indeed, the second her foot touched the slimy stones of the docks, a roguishly handsome man, dressed in clothes immaculate but stiff from sea salt, stepped forward.

"My sincerest congratulations, your Grace," the captain said with a smile. It took Liv a moment to understand that it was she he was addressing. She was a Duchess now; the thought gave her no joy.

"Thank you, Captain -?"

"Black," the man helpfully supplied.

"My biggest fear in life, was that I would marry a man called Black," Liv confessed with a smile, for the handsome rogue had a most charming disposition, that invited secrets. "For then I would have gone from Olive Greene to Olive Black, and I would never have lived it down."

"Have no fear, your Grace," Captain Black said, with an amused glance at the Duke who was glaring at him angrily, a simmering mountain of jealous rage, "His Grace would never give you over to another man, now that you are his."

"Is the cargo loaded?" Ruan interjected, tired, it seemed, of all the niceties, and wishing to break the two apart.

The Duke and the Captain descended into conversation about the load in the cargo hold, the currents in the Avon Gorge, and the weather expected once they were at sea. Liv trailed behind them along the dock, feeling quite at sea herself. She had never visited this part of Bristol, it being reserved for sailors and the working classes, not gently born ladies. She gazed about in awe, at the plethora of activities going on around her. Men moved about, not caring if they jostled or knocked into her, which some did. There were so many of them, all brown, freckled or alarmingly red from the strong sun, and a lot of them appeared to be missing half their teeth, she noted with alarm. And then her eyes fell upon The Seven Stars Inn, and she knew why so many sailors were making their way in that direction. For in the building next door to the pub, disreputable ladies leaned out the windows waving silken scarves, trying to entice the men inside.

A brothel.

Liv flushed, and stole a glance at her husband, wondering if he had ever sought pleasure there. As though feeling her gaze upon his broad back, the Duke stopped and turned to look at her.

"This is ours," he nodded to the huge vessel, docked at the berth, a proud expression on his face.

"It's rather large," Liv answered, wondering what on earth she was supposed to say about his ship. Was it like a carriage or a phaeton? Did men seek endless compliments on its form and structure, as though it was an extension of their own self? Liv had been bored to tears, during her short season, by men obsessed with their vehicles —she hoped her husband was not of the same ilk.

"Of course, it's large," the Duke's sensuous mouth quirked with amusement. "It's a ship. Come."

To her surprise, and Captain Black's delight, the Duke walked over to her purposefully and hauled her up into his arms.

"W-what are you doing?" Liv asked, as cat calls sounded out around them. The feeling of being pressed so close against his chest was most disconcerting, and for a minute she was glad that he held her in his arms, for her legs would have given out beneath her at the dizzy sensation that had overtaken her.

"I'm carrying you over the threshold," Ruan said, glancing down at her with blue eyes that sparkled with amusement. He knew that she was uncomfortable, and the wretch found it entertaining.

"It's not necessary, your Grace," Liv protested, to no avail. "I can walk."

"I've told you, wife dearest," Ruan dropped his head to whisper in her ear, his voice menacing and soft, his breath tickling her sensitive skin. "You must call me Ruan."

"Ruan," Liv echoed faintly.

He carried her up the gangplank, as though she weighed no more than a sack of coal. The crew of The Elizabeth, being too well trained to wolf whistle, saluted as he strode across the deck and kicked the door open to the small hallway which led to the cabins.

"Here we are."

Ruan let her down gently, his hand reaching out to steady her as Liv stumbled. The floor was solid, but it rocked from the lapping waves that jostled the boat; a queer, unsteady feeling she had never experienced. The cabin was large enough, and scrupulously clean. There were no decorative items, just a bed, a small chest of drawers, as well as a table and chair.

"It's lovely," she offered, idly wondering where her portmanteau had got to. The battered, leather bag was the only thing she had left of home, and in it she had stuffed the few items of clothing she possessed alongside a miniature of her mother. A sad collection of belongings for a woman of three and twenty.

"It's not lovely," Ruan growled, waving a dismissive hand at the cabin. "But it's clean, and it will get you safely to France, where you shall have any luxury your heart desires."

Liv wondered when her new husband would notice that her heart did not desire luxuries, diamonds, or dresses. He had taken her home from her, ripped her away from the village she had grown up in and utterly destroyed any tenuous shred of love she had left for her father. He had ruined her, as surely as he had ruined every other life he decided to play with, and now he was expecting her to be pleased that her miserable days would be spent in luxurious surroundings.

"Thank you, your Grace," she said, through gritted teeth, turning to inspect the cabin further.

"I've told you," he came up behind her, spinning her around so that she faced him, "To call me Ruan."

He was huge, the tip of her head just reached his chest, and she had to lean back so that she could look him in the eyes.

"It's an apt name," she whispered, her heart pounding with a mixture of fear and desire. She had never found a man to be so compellingly attractive as the Duke of Everleigh. His features were perfection, ice blue eyes, framed by thick black lashes, a straight aristocratic nose and a mouth so beautiful it was almost cruel.

He is cruel, she reminded herself sternly, though her body had melted at just one brief touch.

"Aye," the Duke whispered softly, his hand snaking around her waist, and pulling her against his chest. "It is an apt name, for a man such as I. But I mean it when I say, I will do you no harm. Not now, not ever."

He didn't give her a chance to respond, instead his lips crashed against hers, hungrily demanding her acquiescence. His mouth was soft, but his kisses were hard and rough, and despite herself Olive found that she was rising to his challenge. His tongue probed her soft mouth, and she allowed him to do so, not willing to betray how unprepared she was for this moment. Her body, despite her brain's protests, reacted in ways she had never felt. Her bosom ached as it pressed against his chest, and when he reached around to cup her bottom with a low, guttural growl, her insides melted. He could conquer her completely, and she would readily give in to the onslaught of pleasure.

"Enough," with what seemed like a huge force of effort, the Duke broke away from her, his breath heavy, panting. Olive remained rigid, standing still on the spot. Her cheeks were flushed with a combination of shame and desire – some fight she had put up against her new husband. One kiss and she melted like butter in the sun.

"I'll not take you on a boat," Ruan muttered, looking distressed. His face was a picture of agony, and from his breeches, Olive could spot the exact source of his pain.

"I'll not take you on a boat," he said again, in tones more decisive. He walked over to her and cupped her face with his large, rough hands. His eyes held hers for a moment, before he kissed her again, this time softly and slowly, as though he sought to savour the moment. He pressed against her lightly, and lifted his lips from her own, tracing hot kisses along her neck.

"When we couple Olive," he whispered promisingly in her ear, "We'll not leave our bed for a month. You have my word."

Olive ached with longing, her body totally ensnared by him. His strong arms held her tight, whilst his lips explored the virgin skin of her sensitive neck.

"Make sail!"

A roar from on deck wrenched them both from each other, and Ruan ran a distracted hand through his thick hair. He looked most disconcerted – perhaps he hadn't planned on kissing her at all.

"I'll send someone down with tea and salt cakes," he said, straightening his coat, which had become slightly rumpled in their frantic tussle.

"They're plain, but they'll keep you from casting up your accounts, if the feeling arises."

"Wonderful," Liv whispered, unable to look him in the eye. She was ashamed that she had responded to him with such wanton need. Where were her reserves of strength and courage? They had fled like frightened sheep in the face of one silly kiss. Well, two, two silly kisses, but that was little consolation.

"If you need anything," the Duke stood at the open door, watching her carefully. "Just call for me."

"I will," Liv removed her pelisse from her shoulders and sat down on the bed, testing the springs with a rather unladylike bounce.

"Don't do that."

The Duke's face looked strained.

"Do what?" perplexed, Liv finally met his eye.

"Bounce around on the bed like that," he growled, "Or I'll renege on my vow to leave you alone 'till we reach Paris."

Liv stopped bouncing immediately, at pains to stay stock still. The Duke laughed at the look of contrition on her face, his own face amused yet yearning.

"If you need anything," he said again, before he closed the door, "Just call for me. I'll be down to check on you later, try and get some rest."

With that he was gone, leaving Liv feeling a little bereft. A cabin boy, awed at serving a woman of such high rank, as she now was, left her in a jug of water and some stale looking biscuits.

"We're casting off now, your Grace," he said with a deferential bow as he left the room. "If you feel sick at all, just pace. It helps you find your sea legs and settles your stomach."

Everything was so new, being referred to as "Your Grace", the sudden, persistent rocking of the ship which made her stomach heave, and Ruan. Her new husband.

He seemed so sincere, in his promise to protect her, yet he did not seem to see that it was he who had kidnapped her from the safety of her home, and set her on this path where his protection was required. And who would save her from him?

Liv had never experienced the aching, yearning, hungry desire that the Duke had inspired with just a kiss, and it frightened her. What she longed for, what her heart sought, was to be free of him - for he was dangerous. She was trapped, true in a gold cage, gilded with the promise of unknown pleasure, but trapped none the less with the Duke of Ruin.

The ship lurched as it entered the free waves, and Liv's stomach hurled with a feeling of nausea. She did not like this new life at all, she decided, stuffing a salt biscuit into her mouth and finding that the Duke had been right. It did soothe her.

Ruan stood on the top deck of the brigantine, watching the crew prepare to take her out to sea. As they passed out of the Bristol Channel and into open waters the two square masts were hoisted and the ship's speed picked up. The strong winds were like a cold slap in the face, despite the strength of the sun, which still lingered in the summer sky. Ruan took a deep breath of bracing sea air, to calm himself.

He had always felt at home aboard any sailing vessel. After Oxford his father had given him a stipend, to do with as he pleased. While most of his friends disappeared to London, to gamble and drink their inheritances away, Ruan had invested his money wisely in the merchant trade. His father thought that he was sullying his noble hands, by investing in trade, but after the old codger had died, leaving Ruan with a pile of crumbling, destitute estates, he was glad that he had not listened to the man. He was one of the wealthiest men in England, perhaps nearly as wealthy as Prinny himself, and he took pride in all that he had accomplished.

The ship lurched, and Ruan grabbed hold of the rails to steady himself. He was a man of vision, a man capable of using ruthless means to attain what he wanted. Just look at his new wife; he had suffered no fits of consciousness when he set out to win her hand. But now that he had it... Ruan cursed into the wind. He owned her now, legally she was his, but then Olive's green, accusing eyes had let him know that he might have power over her body, but never her spirit. And what a spirited woman she was. Ruan's loins ached at the memory of how she had met every challenging kiss and caress, with her own. It had been wild, rough, verging on violent – it had also been completely unplanned.

Ruan had meant to woo Olive into his bed, but he had behaved like boorish fool, pawing at her with an insatiable lust the second the door had closed on her cabin. It shook him to his very core; he prided himself on being aloof. On being in control.

"Winds should pick up past Cornwall, your Grace."

The Captain came to stand beside him, mimicking his stance by leaning forward, his elbows balanced on the rails, his gaze focused on the horizon.

"Do you think we'll out run the storm?"

Ruan asked this casually, for he had no fear of a small storm off the English coast, having suffered far worse on his trips to the Americas. The calm seas of Europe were positively polite to sailors in comparison to the rough Atlantic.

"Aye, we should," Black shrugged, his face unreadable. "And if we don't, no worry. She's a strong ship, your Grace, best I've ever captained."

The Elizabeth was the latest acquisition to Ruan's ever expanding fleet. A sturdy vessel that could carry nearly two-hundred tonnes of cargo – she would serve him well. The seas of Europe had opened once more to trade now Napoleon was defeated, and Ruan intended to capitalise on the new investment opportunities. At the time the war had taken a slight toll on his income, but it had also gifted him with talented men like Captain Black, who had become unemployed once war had ended.

"I did not know you were seeking a wife," his young Captain said, after a short silence, watching him from the corner of his eye.

"I'm sorry I didn't tell you Black, but you're not my type anyway. You were never in the running, so don't feel too hard done by." Ruan replied dryly. The younger man was a mystery to him, he spoke with the clipped, bored tones of the aristocracy – yet claimed no connection. He had captained one of the navy's largest ships during the Napoleonic wars, a feat which would normally have required the purchase of a large commission, but Captain Black, from Plymouth seemed to have worked his way up to the top of the food-chain through sheer grit and determination. A feat Ruan admired.

"If I am honest, Captain," he said thoughtfully, his eyes still on the horizon. "The sudden urge to secure my line, overcame me."

Captain Black snorted, and even Ruan gave a rueful smile, for he had worded that badly.

"I think someone is trying to kill me," he said bluntly, watching for his employee's reaction. "And as such, I thought it prudent that I find a wife to give me a son, so the line doesn't die out with me."

"How romantic," Black quipped, then seemed to remember he was speaking with a superior, and quickly apologised. "What makes you think someone is trying to kill you, your Grace?"

"The bolts on the wheel of my carriage were loosened a few weeks ago" Ruan said gravely, beginning to list the many mishaps that had occurred of late. "I was stabbed by a footpad, in Covent Garden. I fed one of my dogs a side of beef, that was intended for me, and the poor thing died in agony."

Captain Black winced and Ruan allowed himself a grimace; that had been a truly awful night, watching his beloved Wolfhound suffer.

"Do you have any idea, your Grace, who it might be?"

"The list of men who wish me dead, is very long, I assure you." Ruan said with a dark laugh. "T'would be easier to make a list of men who don't wish me to the devil."

"You don't think it's me though," Black stated, awarding him with a grin.

"Why do you say that?" Ruan asked, though he was right. There was something inherently honest and good about Captain Black; one could tell that he lived by a strong code of ethics that he strictly imposed on himself, and that he would rather die than act dishonourably.

"Well, you wouldn't be telling me all this," Black smiled, "If you thought that I was the perpetrator."

"True."

In truth, Ruan hadn't told anyone about his suspicions. He had thought, at the beginning, that he was going mad, but the grim look on Black's face told him that he was right; someone was trying to murder him.

"Shall we toast to your new marriage?" Black suggested; they were rounding Land's End, the green hills of Cornwall still visible in the distance. Soon they would push into the English Channel, and they would reach France by dawn.

"At this moment in time, I couldn't think of anything better than a drink," Ruan agreed, thinking that he had best stay above deck because he would be too tempted to bed Olive below. Both men had turned from the rails, to make their way to the slop, when a loud explosion rocked the vessel, sending them sprawling to the floor.

"What was that?" Ruan roared, scrambling to his feet to assess the damage.

"Felt like a bloody cannon ball, your Grace," Black shouted in response, already running to the lower deck to see what had happened.

"Some of the cargo has exploded in the main hold, Cap'n," a petrified crew member said, as both men reached the lower deck. "It's ripped through the hull, and she's takin' on water fast. We'll nae manage to save her."

"What are we carrying?" Ruan asked his captain, urgently.

"Skeins of exploding cotton, apparently," the younger man replied, his mouth a grim line. "It looks like whoever's trying to kill you doesn't care who gets in the way. Go and fetch her Grace, and meet back here by the small boats. I'll have to go downstairs to see if we can save her, before I give the orders to evacuate."

Olive.

Ruan cursed savagely, and ran to the stairs which led below deck. As he moved through the dark hallway, the acrid stench of smoke assaulted his nose, causing him to cough and splutter. The cargo of cotton would act like kindling to a fire, and it would not be long until the whole ship was aflame.

"Olive," he shouted, banging on the door of her cabin, which seemed to be wedged shut.

"Your Grace?"

Her voice, muffled through the closed door, sounded frightened. Ruan scowled at the way she addressed him, but now was not the time for a lecture on showing wifely affection.

"Is the door locked?" he roared, pulling the front of his coat over his moth and nose, for smoke was now billowing heavily through the corridor.

"No," Olive shouted, apparently kicking the door for it rattled on its hinges. "It's wedged stuck, it must have been from the force of the blast."

"Stand back," Ruan ordered, taking a large step back before throwing his full weight against the door. It moved slightly, but did not budge. Annoyed he tried again, and this time the weight of his shoulder shattered the door to splinters. He vaguely registered shooting pain, but his main concern was getting to Olive, and then getting her safely off the ship before it was engulfed in flames.

"Come," he coughed, grabbing her hand to guide her out.

"My bag," she spluttered, for by speaking she had inhaled a lungful of smoke.

"No time," Ruan spoke tersely, dragging her forcibly from the room. He led the way down the dark corridor, both crouching low agianst the billowing smoke. When they emerged on deck, they gasped simultaneously, willing their lungs to be filled with fresh, sea air.

"Oh, goodness."

Olive's gaze was fixated on the masts. The foremast was ablaze, burning as hot as the fires of hell, and its sails were whipping against the larger main mast, which looked set to go up in flames in seconds.

"Get to a small boat," Ruan instructed, but too late he realised that there were none there, for the whole front of the ship was burning.

"Can you swim?" he asked, grabbing her by the shoulders and shaking her roughly, willing her to understand the urgency of the situation.

"I can," she nodded, her face pale but calm. Silhouetted against the dark night sky, and the burning inferno of the ship, she looked beautiful. Strong, brave and beautiful. But now was not the time for compliments, so instead Ruan dragged her by the arm to the railings of the deck. Their way was precarious, for the front of the ship had begun to sink rapidly, and the deck beneath their feet sloped downward at a sharp angle.

"It will be cold," Ruan warned, kicking of his Hessians, not wanting the heavy leather boots to weigh him down in the water.

Olive nodded, taking a deep, steadying breath.

"I'll go first," he continued, swinging his legs over the rails, "And you follow. I'll catch you, never fear."

He took a deep breath, held his nose and jumped into the freezing cold sea. The icy water shocked the air from his lungs, and for a second Ruan floundered beneath the waves, struggling to break the surface.

Olive, he thought wildly to himself, I have to get to Olive.

Kicking his powerful legs, he propelled himself to the surface of the choppy sea, treading water as he tried to gauge the distance to the ship. It was but a few yards away, and with strong strokes, he swam over to the burning vessel.

"Olive," he called to his wife, who was perched on the railings, evidently paralysed by fear. "Jump."

The main sail had caught fire now, and it was a terrible thing to behold. If she didn't jump she would be burned alive as the wooden ship turned into a bonfire.

"Ruan," she looked out to where he was, and seeing him in the water seemed to bolster her confidence. With a shriek she launched herself into the sea, toward her husband.

Ruan swam to where she had entered the water, fear making him nauseas. She cannot die, he thought frantically, as he scanned the waves. The relief that he felt when he spotted her red hair was palpable. She was alive, and she had not lied, she was a strong swimmer.

"We must try to get to the small boats."

Ruan spoke urgently, tugging at her hand to pull her in the direction of the stern of the ship, where surely some of the small boats would be. The night was dark, but the glow of the fire illuminated the inky black sea. He saw her eyes flash, and though her teeth chattered, Olive wore a look of steely determination.

Man and wife began to swim toward the sound of voices, which echoed above the roar of the burning ship. We'll be safe, Ruan thought happily, Black will not leave until each and every crew member is accounted for. This was the last thought he would have for the rest of the night, for with an ominous creak, the pole holding up the main mast shattered, and crashed into the sea. A stray piece of rigging hit Ruan's skull with such force that it rendered him unconscious, and he was drifting into blackness, sinking below the waves.

"Ruan."

His name was ripped from her chattering lips while Liv watched in horror as the main mast came crashing into the sea. Her husband disappeared from view, and, frantically, Liv swam toward the burning piece of wood, desperate to save him.

She spotted his white shirt, as he sank, slowly, down toward the deep bed. Taking a lungful of air, Liv dived beneath the waves, kicking her legs with a strength she had not known she possessed. Thank goodness, her mother had insisted she learn how to swim. Lila Green had grown up by the ocean in Devon, and had lost two brothers during a freak boating accident. As such, she had insisted that Olive received lessons, despite it being a less than lady like endeavour. Liv had not been in the water since before her teens, but the instinct to kick was unconscious, almost like breathing. The salty water stung her eyes, as she clawed her way toward Ruan. Her lungs began to burn, and her mind screamed at her to seek the surface, but she persisted. She reached out, found Ruan's limp hand, and with a final burst of energy she kicked upward, her ears ringing in panic.

Finally, after what felt like an eternity, she found air.

"Oh, God," she whimpered, inhaling deep, deep, lung-fulls of precious air. She hooked one arm around her husband's torso, allowing the water to take his weight, so that he floated against her.

"Ruan," she whimpered, looking at his blank face. He was breathing, thank goodness, though completely unconscious.

"Help," Liv called out, hoping that somewhere in the distance, someone might hear her. The ship was ablaze, and Liv could see the small boats, containing the evacuated crew, but they were too far away to see them. Her dress was sodden, heavy and cumbersome, and when she tried to swim one handed, still supporting Ruan, toward them, she swallowed a mouth full of salt water that left her gagging. She sank beneath the waves, and had to claw her way back to the floating position she had held before.

Swimming toward the crew meant swimming against the current, whereas the tide was naturally pulling them toward the shore, she reasoned in an attempt to calm herself. She was usually level headed, but the weight of Ruan was making her panic, though even she could be forgiven for becoming overwrought given the current circumstances, she thought.

If I swim with the current, it will be easier than fighting it, she decided. The shore was not that far away, small dots of light – presumably cottages – were visible, and though Ruan was large, the water took most of his weight. It was arduous, it took over an hour, and at many stages Liv contemplated simply letting go of the Duke, for she feared that if she held onto him, she herself would drown. Finally, exhausted, freezing and on the verge of tears, she reached the sandy shore of a small cove. Hoisting the Duke onto the beach was no mean feat. In the water he had been almost weightless, but on dry land he was extraordinarily heavy.

"Why did I have to marry such a beast of a man?" Liv groaned, as she dragged the Duke across the small beach they had washed up on. It was nestled at the bottom of two sloping hills, and tucked in the middle of these, was a small fisherman's cottage. Light blazed cheerfully from the windows, and when she finally reached it, Liv found the door was ajar.

"Hello?" she called, laying Ruan down, to dash inside and look for help. But when she entered, the small front-room was empty; the fire burned in the hearth, and on the table lay a half-eaten supper. The occupants of the cottage must have seen The Elizabeth, and rushed to help. Chilled to the bone, and shaking slightly, Liv retraced her steps, and dragged her husband inside.

"You're so heavy," she whispered, half in annoyance, as she hauled him into the warmth. He was still completely unconscious, and she knew that she needed to divest him of his wet clothes straight away, before he caught a chill.

Laying him on the rug before the fire, Liv removed his jacket and shirt quickly, but hesitated when she got to his breeches.

You are his wife, a voice in her head taunted, but despite this fact, Liv felt too nervous to confront her husband's nether regions just then, and instead threw a blanket over him to protect his modesty, before yanking his trousers off. It was a difficult task, for the sodden cloth was stuck to his skin, and his thighs were large and muscular, but eventually he was undressed. Only when she was certain that her husband was comfortable, did Liv strip off her own wet dress and undergarments. She wrapped herself in a blanket, stolen from the adjacent bedroom, and hunkered down by the fire, beside the slumbering Ruan.

He was beautiful; even with his eyes closed he had the face of an Adonis. Liv reached out, and ran her hand over his hair, checking for lumps, bumps or bleeding. Ruan groaned at her touch, which she took as a good sign – at least he could feel. His hand, which rested above the blanket, showed signs of growing chilblains. His fingers were becoming swollen and red, and Liv noticed that on his index finger he wore a signet ring, around which the skin was becoming angrily bloated.

She slid it from his finger, and placed it on her own thumb for safe keeping, thinking that it would be a pity if, after all her heroics, he would lose a finger because of a ring. Satisfied that her husband would live, Olive threw another log on the fire, to keep it burning. She stood up and wandered over to the table, snatching a piece of bread from the cottage owner's abandoned supper, and stuffing it greedily into her mouth. She was ravenous after her hours in the water. Once her stomach was full, she peeked out the front door, gazing toward the sea.

In the distance the lights of many boats surrounded the smouldering wreckage of The Elizabeth, twinkling bravely in the darkness. Liv said a quiet, fervent prayer that the crew might be rescued safely.Then there was nought for her to do, but wait, so she returned to the chair beside the fire and promptly fell asleep.

A grey dawn was breaking, when she woke with a start. For a second she could not place where she was, until she recalled the events from the night before. Ruan was still slumbering, under his blankets. His face, she was glad to see, looked much healthier. His cheeks had colour, and he now looked to be asleep, rather than on the verge of death. A small fire still burned in the grate, and Olive threw another log on, wondering what was keeping the owner of the cottage from returning. Perhaps they were salvaging cargo from the ship, for this was the south of England, and people weren't above wrecking ships for profit, so a naturally sunk vessel would be seen as fair game.

Her clothes, which she had laid out on a chair beside the fire were now dry; stiff from sea salt and warm to the touch.

She hastily donned her chemise, and petticoats, and slipped her red dress over her head. Her slippers, no longer wet, were a sorry sight, but better than nothing. Once clothed, she went in search of a privy, for the pressing need of her bladder was what had woken her from her deep slumber.

She cast a glance at Ruan as she tiptoed past him. Even after the events of the night before, he was still but a stranger to her. This unwelcome interlude in their travels would soon end, and she would once more be facing the prospect of a life as his wife. She remembered the searing passion that he had kissed her with, and she shivered. From fear or desire, she could not tell, but it unsettled her none the less and so she hurried past him, overcome by the need to escape.

Like most country abodes, the privy was situated outside. Liv quickly went about her business, for the small shed was cold and filled with spiders. As she walked across the yard back to the cottage, she heard the sound of voices from within, and paused mid-step.

"Wonder 'ow 'e got in?" a deep male voice said, in a Cornish twang.

"Aye," another voice, this time female agreed, "And 'ow 'e managed to strip 'imself of all 'is clothes. Not that I'm complainin', for 'e's a fine looking gentleman without 'em."

"Hush wife," the male voice admonished, sounding more amused than annoyed. Liv peeked through the gap in the door, and saw an older couple standing by the fire, peering at Ruan curiously.

"Look," the bent old woman cried, pointing a gnarled finger, "'E's waking up!"

Liv held her breath, as Ruan groaned. She could see him struggling to sit upright, his handsome face awash with confusion.

"Who are you? How did I get here?" His tone was haughty as ever, evidently the blow to his head had done his ego no harm.

"We were about to ask you the same question," the old man said with a deep laugh. "Did you come off The Elizabeth? You'll be glad to know the crew are all safe, if you did, but they're missing a Duke."

"I am the Duke of Everleigh."

From her vantage point, Liv saw Ruan scramble unsteadily to his feet, clutching the blanket around his waist, to protect his modesty. He towered above the old couple, his bare chest bronze and breathtakingly powerful.

"How did I get here?" he repeated imperiously, startling the old couple, "And is there any news of my wife?"

That was all Liv needed to hear.

Nobody knows if I'm alive or dead, she thought silently to herself, and while most people would have found that slightly morbid, Live felt a sudden lightness in her soul.

I'm free.

A voice in her head sang a hallelujah, as her mind began to form a plan. She would go to the nearest village, pawn the ring she had taken from her husband's finger, and set up a new life elsewhere.Quickly, before doubt began to set in, she turned and fled, scrambling up the hill away from the cottage and the Duke of Ruin.

You can't just let him think you sank to a watery grave, her conscience nagged at her, as she traipsed along the steep hill path. And though her conscience was right, in that it was a heartless act, Olive remained resolute.

She owed Ruan Ashford nothing, she thought bitterly. He had stolen her life away from her, for his own amusement and pleasure. Her faith in her father, her childhood home and friends had all disappeared at the click of his arrogant fingers - she might as well be dead.

And now I am, she thought with a small smile.

"She's not dead."
Ruan looked Captain Black calmly in the eye, as he took a deep swig of his pint of ale. They were seated in a dark tavern, near Packet Quays in Falmouth. The Captain had just surmised exactly what had become of The Elizabeth and her crew. All men were accounted for bar one, a new tar that had joined up at Bristol; the missing man was the chief suspect in what Ruan knew to be yet another attempt on his life. Other men had reported seeing him go down to the main hold just minutes before the explosion, and as cotton wasn't liable to blow up on its own, they had deduced that he had been the one to set it alight. Captain Black had been in the middle of outlining how the crew were going about searching for Olive, who they presumed lost at sea, when the Duke had interrupted him.

"She's not dead," he repeated again, though he could see doubt in the other man's dark eyes. "I know you think I'm mad, but I didn't manage to wake up in a cottage, naked as the day I was born through divine intervention. God doesn't like me enough for that. It was Olive, she brought me there."

Ruan was certain of it. He remembered little of the previous night, bar the horrifying moment that the mast had crashed down upon his head, and another hazy recollection of someone stroking his hair. When he had woken up in the fisherman's cottage, embarrassingly nude and disorientated, he had not been able to recollect how he had arrived there. His clothes had been laid out before the hearth to dry, and the fire within had burned merrily, despite the long absence of the fisherman and his wife. There was no way that he had managed to do all that when he had been rendered completely unconscious. It had to have been the work of his wife.

"Beg your pardon, your Grace," Black interjected, his expression troubled, "But if it was Her Grace who dragged you all the way to the shore, then why did she disappear after?"

"Probably because she knew that everyone would assume she had perished," Ruan replied evenly, taking another sip of the slightly warm ale, and grimacing at its bitterness. "She wasn't exactly enamoured at the thought of being my wife - perhaps she simply seized the opportunity that was presented to her."

"She can't have simply decided to disappear," Black laughed nervously, evidently uncomfortable with his employer's brutal honesty. "Perhaps she was in shock? I'll have the men search the beaches and the cliffs, in case she wandered in a daze."

"She wasn't in shock," Ruan sighed in annoyance, and set his now empty glass on the table. "A woman in shock wouldn't have had the mental capacity to take my signet ring on her way out the door."

Black's own face was a perfect picture of shock at this news, his mouth hanging open in a round "O" of surprise.

"You'll catch flies like that," Ruan grunted, and the young man immediately snapped his mouth shut.

"So what you're saying," Black said slowly, as though his mind were still trying to digest what Ruan had told him, "Is that Her Grace, rescued you from drowning and then disappeared. Purposefully."

"That's about the sum of it, yes," Ruan agreed, waving for the tavern-wench to refill his glass. He did not know how to feel about Olive's desertion; yes it pricked at his pride, but another part of him admired her temerity. She was feisty, and brave, two of the exact reasons he had married her. His loins stirred at the memory of the way that she had responded to his kisses; she had been unsure and innocent, but even that had not stopped her from reciprocating his passion. Ruan growled in annoyance, he had nearly had her but had been too gentlemanly to bed her on a ship. Well, that wouldn't happen the next time he saw her. Even if they met in a hay-barn, he would throw her down on the straw and make her his completely —chivalry be damned.

"What's the plan from here, your Grace?"

The young Captain interrupted his thoughts, which had drifted to rather licentious images of Olive, tousled and wanton on a bed of hay.

"Find her," Ruan cleared his throat, and tried to look more controlled than he felt. "Offer a reward for her capture. One thousand pounds. Let it be known at the docks, for she might turn up there looking for passage abroad."

"As you wish," Captain Black inclined his head, though his lips quirked with amusement. "Perhaps though, your Grace, I shall offer the reward for her safe return, and not her capture. It sounds less romantic when you word it that way."

"Romantic?" Ruan arched an eyebrow, "Never heard of the word."

"Well that's obvious enough," Black laughed heartily, and stood to leave, donning his hat. He paused before he left, and gave the Duke a thoughtful look. "It's not all doom and gloom, your Grace."

"And why is that?"

"Well, she could have let you drown..."

Ruan snorted into the fresh ale that had just been set down before him. Captain Black was right; his wife could have left him to drown, and found herself a wealthy widow as a result. It gave him pause for thought; Olive didn't wish him dead, which given his history, was about as romantic as it got.

"Four hundred pounds."

The closed faced man in the pawn shop did not blink, as he offered Liv a most extraordinary amount of money for the ring she had placed on the counter. Her lips parted to say yes, but her whirring mind stopped her before the words could leave her mouth. This was his first offer, and it was obscenely high, surly that meant that the ring was worth more to him than four hundred pounds?

"Seven hundred," she replied boldly, her eyes meeting his. He blinked, and she saw his lip curl in annoyance.

"Madam I could not possibly offer you more than four-fifty," he said, affecting an air of great sadness. Liv bit back a giggle; he was a most remarkable actor, his face portraying genuine regret, though he was overdoing it a tad.

"And I could not possibly accept any less than six-hundred, for such a treasured heirloom."

Her own acting skills were as hammy as the pawn-shop proprietor's. He arched an amused eyebrow, her sentimentality obviously making little impression on his hard nose.

"I'll tell you what, young lady," the man leaned forward on the counter, as though he were going to whisper a secret in her ear. "I'll give you five-hundred, not a penny more, and I won't ask you how you came to be in possession of this ring."

"Deal," Liv replied firmly, her cheeks flushing. Would he call the magistrate? She began to fret and fidget nervously, but she needn't have worried, for the man disappeared into a back room, and came out with a wad of pound notes, which he laboriously counted out on the counter, before handing them to her with a false sigh.

"Thank you, sir," Liv inclined her head toward the man, making to leave.

"No," he gave her a sly smile, "Thank you, young lady. I would have paid double if you'd pushed me."

He waved her away with a laugh, and while for a moment Liv felt as though she'd been cheated, when she exited the shop onto Market Street, a sense of giddy elation overtook her.

Five hundred pounds!

Never, in all her life, had Liv been in possession of such an enormous sum. It was enough to live on for years, she thought happily, skipping into a drapers and purchasing two day-dresses, a pair of sturdy boots, a fresh set of undergarments and a bag to hold them all. She was ready to begin her new life, the only trouble on the horizon being that she had no idea where to go.

As she strolled down toward Packet Quays, where Falmouth Packet ships filled the harbour, she fell into step behind two sailors. They were of the merchant navy, wearing the bleached clothes of tars, but among the crowds Liv also spotted a few gentlemen in impressive, uniforms, their gold buttons gleaming in the sun. Falmouth was one of the busiest ports in all of England, and for now she was safe, blending amongst the crowds.

"He's offered a reward of one thousand pounds for the man who finds her," one sailor was saying to the other. Liv's ears pricked with interest, for she had an idea who the unnamed man they were speaking of was.

"A thousand pound?" the other sailor exclaimed. "If I'd a thousand pounds to throw away I'd spend it on one thousand lightskirts, not one miserable wife."

His friend guffawed appreciatively, whilst Liv resisted rolling her eyes.

"No one'll find her," the first sailor said with a shrug, "She drowned as far as I can see. That's two dead wives now, by my count. Wonder if he staged the whole thing, to hide the fact that he killed this one too?"

The men descended into a deep conversation, about the peculiarities of the aristocracy, which Liv half listened to as she trailed them to the Quays. If Ruan had offered a reward for her safe return, then surely she was not safe here, she had to leave as quickly as possible.

At Packet Quays, where mailboats from every corner of the British Empire docked, there was a plethora of stagecoaches to chose from.

"Which one is leaving first?" Liv asked of the man at the office of the stagecoach company. The bald headed man looked over at a driver, who was imbibing a large tankard of ale on a wooden bench.

"'Ere Greg," the man called, and the driver looked up, his face a picture of unhappiness. "When's you leavin'?"

"In about ten minutes," the driver gave a dark scowl. "Just waiting on my passenger to finish their business."

The fearful way that he spoke of his missing passenger, made Liv think that he was ferrying a hardened criminal through the Cornish countryside. Reluctantly she bought a ticket to St. Jarvis, which was where the coach was headed, thinking that it was best to make her escape quickly, even if she had to share her carriage with a deviant.

Ten minutes later, Liv boarded the rickety, old carriage, that was to take her to her new home. She looked longingly at the other, well sprung vehicles which lined the road, but they were reserved for passengers headed to London, or Bristol; St. Jarvis seemed decidedly more low key.

After a minute alone in the dark compartment, the door was opened by the driver, who ushered his wayward passenger inside. Liv steeled herself, expecting a coarse drunkard or a light-skirt, but instead she found herself looking at a young, bespectacled woman, who blinked at her owlishly from behind her glasses.

"Why, hello," the young woman said earnestly. In her hands she held a broadsheet, which had left her fingers covered in ink, and her nose was covered with similar black smudges. "The driver said I'd have a companion for the rest of the trip. I've been sitting up front with him since Truro. He was completely fascinated by a paper I'm writing on the moralities of the Romans, but insisted I keep you company for the rest of the journey. I've promised him I shall post him a copy of my essay when it's done."

The woman beamed, though her smile faltered a little, when the driver took off with great speed, causing her to fall backwards onto her seat. Liv bit back a grin, so this was the wayward passenger that had made Greg the driver so unhappy. He did not seem like a man who would be interested in anyone's morals, let alone those of a long dead civilisation; the woman had obviously missed her target audience.

"Jane Deveraux," she said to Liv with a smile, holding out her hand to shake, but then glanced down and gave a howl of dismay as she saw that it was black with ink.

"Oh, dear," she sighed, taking out a hankie and wiping her grubby digits, "I'm afraid I'm always doing this. Usually I wait until I'm home alone to read the papers, but the headline today was so interesting, that I just had to read it straight away."

Olive paled, she had an inkling what the main story in the Falmouth Daily Chronicles was.

"Elizabeth Sinks: New Duchess Missing," the young woman read breathlessly. She looked up at Liv, her wide eyes looking almost bug-like behind her bottle-top glasses. "How awful. Poor Everleigh, I never did believe that he killed his first wife."

"Do you know him?" Liv asked with surprise, for her new companion did not have the look of someone who mixed with the gentry.

"Oh yes," the woman nodded so earnestly, that her glasses fell down her nose. She propped them back up with her finger, and when she took her hand away her nose was black with ink. "His Cornish estate lies not fifty miles away from my family's. He was close with my brother when they were young, and is a great supporter of a charity I am involved in, which educates young girls."

Liv smiled faintly at this; she had not pegged Ruan as a charitable sort of man.

"Are you visiting with family in St. Jarvis?" the girl asked, changing the subject away from the missing Duchess. "If you are I might know them, I know everyone in the village!"

"Not exactly," Liv replied, trying to sound honest despite the fact she was lying through her teeth. "My husband died, a short time ago, drowned at sea. I am seeking to make a new life, and St. Jarvis was suggested to me as a safe place for a woman alone to live."

This was made-up balderdash of course, but Jane beamed at her praise of the village.

"Oh it is," Miss Devereaux nodded sincerely, "It has always been a haven for young women, ever since the novelist Mrs Baker opened her boarding house. Such a pity she has passed, for in the summer months it was filled with women of an intellectual temperament and guest speakers giving lectures."

"And is the boarding house now closed?" Liv asked curiously, for she recalled having heard of Mrs Baker, one of the original, trailblazing Bluestockings of the previous century. Liv had not known that she had retired to Cornwall, but then she did not run with the intellectual set. She didn't run with any set at all.

"Yes," Jane responded sadly, "My brother fears he will never let it out, and the village misses the boarders, for they brought a lot of money to the local shops."

She sighed, and looked out the window, overcome by melancholy at the loss of Mrs Baker. Liv, on the other hand, smiled at this little nugget of information. She had five-hundred pounds in her purse, but needed a job as it wouldn't last forever. Running a boarding house was bound to be hard work, but Liv was undaunted.

"Do you think your brother would be interested in letting the property to me? I should like to carry on with Mrs Baker's mission, for I was a most ardent admirer of her work." She spoke slowly, hoping that her expression did not betray how much she wanted Jane to say yes, whilst also praying that Jane would not wish to discuss any of Mrs Baker's novels. Liv's reading preferences tended toward the Gothic, which though not very high-brow, were most entertaining.

Her companion blinked happily at her question, and bounced up and down on her seat with excitement.

"Oh, oh, oh," Jane gasped, clapping her hands with glee. "Oh, that's just the most perfect idea. We shall ask Julian the second we arrive. He couldn't possibly say no. Although..."

Jane trailed off uncomfortably, her cheeks flushing.

"What's wrong?" Liv reached out and took the other woman's hand in her own, for she looked most flustered at the mention of her brother.

"It's just, my brother detests bluestockings, he thinks my mixing with Mrs Baker is the reason that I remain unwed - despite my enormous dowry." she confided, "And if he thought that you were going to carry on housing them in St. Jarvis, I'm afraid he might say no."

"Then we shall lie," Liv said firmly, what was another fib on top of the ones she had already told? Jane broke out into another grin at this news, and Liv had the definite feeling that she and the young Miss Deveraux were going to become as thick as thieves.

"How wonderful Mrs - oh, I'm sorry I never caught your name."

"It's Olive," Liv replied automatically, without thinking. She cringed inwardly, why had she not prepared for this part of her tale? If she was going to start a new life, she would obviously have to adopt a new moniker, to go with her assumed identity.

"Olive Black," she finished lamely, for Jane had been waiting for her to speak her surname, and that was the only one that would form on her panicked tongue.

"That's so funny," Jane said distractedly, and Olive waited for her to make a joke about the fruit, but instead she reached for the newspaper that she had cast aside. "The missing wife of the Duke of Everleigh was called Olive Greene, what a coincidence!"

Liv gave a nervous laugh so high pitched she thought that it might summon a pack of dogs.

"How strange," she agreed with her new friend Jane, "But unlike the poor Duchess of Everleigh, I was not lost at sea."

I was found there instead, she thought with a triumphant smile.

Julian Deveraux, Viscount Jarvis, was not what Liv had expected from his sister's description of him. In her mind's eye, she had pictured him as a fussy, older gentleman, but the young man who greeted her was handsome, and no more than thirty years.

Jane had insisted that she visit with Julian straight away, in their home on the edge of the quaint village of St. Jarvis. It was only as the two women were walking up the sweeping drive to the imposing house, that Liv had realised that Jane Deveraux's family were aristocrats. Judging by the size of the Palladian fronted mansion, they were very well to do aristocrats.

Liv had felt a moment of panic when she was introduced to the Viscount, what if Lord Deveraux recognised her from her season in town? But she needn't have worried, for it soon became apparent that they young blood thought of little bar himself. A shy, wallflower like Olive, would not have caught his attention in Almack's - if he ever deigned to attend. For, Lord Deveraux did not have the look of a man who would willingly attend the stuffy assembly. He had the look of a Rake.

"This is my good friend Mrs Black."

Jane made the introduction, beaming at Olive, while her handsome brother regarded her with a surly expression.

"Mrs Black is most interested in opening up the vacant boarding house," Jane continued, her face flushing somewhat. She was not a good liar, Liv deduced, for her expression betrayed her nerves.

"Is that so?"

Lord Deveraux arched an eyebrow, and his dark gaze raked Olive from head to toe, in a most impudent manner.

"Yes," Olive decided that the best way to treat a man like Julian, was to speak firmly, adopting the same tone that one would use with an unruly child. "Your sister has informed me, that you are struggling to find someone to take up the lease, and that as a result the village is suffering."

Julian scowled at his sister, presumably for underselling the value of the boarding house. Jane flushed again, and refused to meet his eye, instead opting to stare fixedly at the carpet on the floor of the library.

"It's a fine building, one of the grandest in the whole village," he declared, his gaze challenging Liv to disagree.

"I should hope so," she replied sweetly, adopting a sickly sweet tone of innocence underscored with a steely note. "For I mean to build a thriving business, my Lord, and should hate to start off in anything less than perfect."

Lord Deveraux gave a harrumph of annoyance, he was not a man who liked women dictating to him, and Liv's confident tone seemed to be upsetting him.

Good, she thought to herself, for she did not like this Lord Deveraux. The way that he spoke to his sister was dismissive and rude, and he was faring no better with Liv. She knew instinctively that a man like Julian would like all women to live by the rule of being seen and not heard, but Liv didn't give a fig. She lived by her own rules now.

"The lease is worth fifty pounds a year," Deveraux snapped, clearly tired of the charade.

"I'll give you thirty," Liv smiled, "For as I understand the building has lain idle for some time, and will be in need of considerable repairs."

"Thirty? I might as well give it away for that price."

"I'd be more than willing to accept that offer too, my Lord," she gave him a glacial stare. "The village is suffering from a lack of visitors, it would be terrible if I was to let it be known in the tavern that you refused a poor, young widow's request to reopen it."

Jane, standing behind her brother, gave Liv a shocked smile. She had probably never witnessed anyone stand up to his bullying.

"Fine," the Viscount growled, raking a hand through his dark hair in agitation. "But I don't want to see it filled with the same riff-raff like that crackpot Mrs Baker entertained."

"I'd hardly call ladies of an intellectual disposition riff-raff," Liv answered evenly. "They're hardly the demimonde."

"Would that they had been," Julian glowered at his sister, who visibly shrank under his censure. "Then maybe dear Jane would have developed an interest in men, like a normal woman, and not dusty old books."

An uncomfortable silence fell, in which Liv regarded the Viscount with what she hoped was a most disapproving look. Poor Jane, red faced, remained silent, her attention still fixated on her feet.

"Call for Edgeford," Julian spoke, after a tense minute. He directed the instruction to his sister, though his eyes still held Liv's. "He'll draw up a lease for this Mrs Black, and then show her to the house."

"Oh Julian, thank you," Jane said, with far too much gratitude and deference to her awful brother for Olive's liking. The young woman took Liv by the hand, and led her to the office of the Viscount's agent John Edgeford, who thankfully had a much more pleasant manner than that of his employer.

"This is it," Edgeford said, as he led both ladies into the dusty entrance hall of the Boarding House, which stood in the centre square of St. Jarvis. It was large, and airy and the walls were covered in delightful little miniatures, which on closer inspection Liv found depicted famous novelists.

"Mrs Baker had no relations," the agent continued, leading Liv and Jane through a maze of rooms, "And so all her things are still here. The pictures, the ornaments, the books..."

Jane gave a squeal of delight as they opened the door to the library, a handsome room lined with mahogany shelves. Every wall was crammed with books, on every different kind of subject; from leather bound works on the Classics, to some very recent Gothic Romances. It appeared the late Mrs Baker had appreciated variety in her reading matter.

"It needs a lot of work," Liv spoke absently to herself as she surveyed the dust, "And I shall have to advertise in the papers that we are open for business again."

"I shall write to the Bas Bleu members tonight," Jane interjected, her glasses sliding down her nose as she smiled with excitement. "They'll spread the word, and we can invite speakers for Wednesday Salons, like Mrs Baker did in the old days. Oh, it shall be such fun!"

Liv had to smile at her enthusiasm, Jane's positive outlook on her current situation bordered on naivety, but her optimism was infectious. Looking around the elegant room, Liv could almost picture in her mind's eye what it would look like filled with fashionably dressed women and men, discussing philosophy and other egalitarian things.

This thought seemed to have crossed Edgeford's mind too, for he looked at Jane frowning, the lines in his forehead even more pronounced with apprehension.

"I don't think your brother would be too happy, if you start trying to resurrect the ghost of Mary Wollstonecraft, Miss Deveraux," he said his tone worried on Jane's behalf. Liv raised an eyebrow at the mention of the controversial writer and philosopher Wollstonecraft, who had been condemned after her death as a fallen woman, for her many affairs and mothering of illegitimate children. Her best known work, A Vindication of the Rights of Women, had shocked the world with its argument that there was no difference between the intelligence of men and women. Liv smiled, of course the bookish Jane would have Wollstonecraft as a heroine.

"Rest assured Mr Edgeford," Liv soothed, "As a widow living alone I should not tolerate anything scandalous happening under my roof, bar tea, cake and enlightened conversation. Which you shall be most welcome to participate in."

Edgeford flushed with pleasure,he was a man in his early fifties, and there had been no mention or hint of a wife or family. The prospect of an evening with pleasant company seemed to cheer him greatly, for he left promising to send up a maid from Lord Deveraux's the next day, to help Olive with the initial clean, and a bucket of coal so they could warm the house.

"Oh, Jane," Liv said, once the older gentleman had left and they were alone in the dusty library, "How can I ever thank you?"

"No, it is I who must thank you Olive," the plain girl replied, breaking into a smile that transformed her face from tired and pinched, to radiant and beautiful. "I can't tell you how happy I am that you are reopening the house. The thought of a summer in St. Jarvis, with no-one for company, why, it was almost unbearable."

Liv longed to ask her new friend about her brother's animosity toward her, and intellectual women in general, but she sensed that now was not the time. The defeated girl who had quailed under her brother's stern disapproval had metamorphosed into a woman filled with energy and light.

"We shall have to find you some help," Jane said, striding from the library and down the hall to the kitchen, "A girl to help with the cleaning and serving at the table, and someone to cook."

"I can cook."

They were in the kitchen now, and even through the gloom - for the shutters were closed on the windows - Liv could see the surprise on Jane's face.

"No really," Olive laughed, as she walked over to the windows and wrenched open the shutters, which creaked and groaned. "I can bake bread, make stews, brew tea. There's no need to hire anyone else yet to do all that, I'm quite adept."

This was true enough, but the knowledge that she would be investing a large portion of her five-hundred pounds into the business made Liv hesitant to hire any staff who might not be needed if the business did not prosper. If the boarding-house made a tidy profit, then perhaps she might hire a cook, for kitchen work was hard, menial and involved rising before dawn.

Specks of dust danced in the light that now streamed through the window, and Liv noted with dismay that the kitchen had fared worst from the house's period of neglect. Apart from the dust, and the dirt, it was a fine big room, with a large wooden table at its centre and a sturdy looking range for cooking.

"It's perfect," she declared, then her smile faltered as a thought struck her. "Apart from the fact that my larder is bare, of course."

Her stomach rumbled loudly as she voiced this concern, and she glanced out the window noting that the sun, while still strong, was definitely preparing to set.

"You can dine at Jarvis House," Jane gamely suggested, but Liv found the idea of eating under the disapproving glare of Lord Deveraux most unappetising. Besides, she rather fancied a few moments alone to take stock of what the day had thrown at her. She was now "widowed", the proprietor of an empty boarding house, and apparently a sponsor of egalitarian thinking. It was all rather a lot to take on board, in just one day.

"Thank you Jane, but I think I shall just fetch some basic provisions for my tea, and then prepare for bed - I'm rather tired after all this excitement!"

And so the two girls walked arm and arm into the village proper, where Jane deposited Liv outside the small general shop, with a promise that when she returned home she would pen a dozen missives to the other ladies of the Bas Bleu Society. Jane bought tea, milk, bread, eggs and butter from the jolly, red-faced man in the shop, who proclaimed himself delighted at the news that the boarding house would reopen, before going home to prepare a rudimentary supper. She did not allow her thoughts return to her husband, until later that night, when she was tucked up in her new bed. Try as she might, the memory of Ruan's searing kiss aboard the ship, and the beauty of his hard muscular body would not leave her head. Liv tossed and turned for hours, until finally she fell into a restless sleep, which was filled with dreams in which she was being hunted by a man, who looked awfully like Ruan.

.

here instead, she thought with a triumphant smile.

"I recognised the crest immediately, your Grace," the owner of the pawn shop on Market Street declared, as he fawned over the signet ring that was laid out on the glass counter. "I was just about to write to your man of business, when I had word that you were in town. How fortunate."

"Indeed," Ruan replied, wondering just how much of a fortune the slippery man opposite him intended to make from the transaction.

He had been staying in Falmouth for the past two days, eagerly awaiting any news on Olive's whereabouts, as well as the whereabouts of the traitorous tar that had blown up The Elizabeth. Cornwall was not a county he frequented often, given the terrible way he had fled five years ago after Catherine's death. Over the past two days however he had found he rather enjoyed being amongst the familiar accents and eccentricities of the local population, not to mention the local ale which tasted just as good as he remembered.

"Who sold it to you?" the Duke asked, as the shop-owner held out the ring for his inspection. Ruan took the heavy, gold piece in his hand, barely glancing at it before he slipped it back upon his index finger. He had worn it every day for a decade, he did not need to examine it minutely to know that it was the Ashford Signet.

"A young woman," the oily man coughed delicately, "She did not seem keen to share her name…"

"And so you never asked it," Ruan growled in reply. "Well, what did she look like?"

"Red hair, and a most bewitching set of green eyes."

Olive.

Ruan heaved a great sigh, and looked at the man opposite him warily. The shop keeper in turn eyed him with a most innocent expression, as though butter wouldn't melt in his mouth.

"How much did you pay the woman for it?"

The shop keeper looked pained, as though speaking of money offended him.

"Nearly eight-hundred pounds, your Grace," he said without blinking.

Ruan resisted rolling his eyes, for he was sure that the price named was an astronomical inflation of what had actually been paid to his wife.

"I shall write to my man of business, and have him send you on what you're owed," he murmured distractedly; he had no time to quibble over money when his wife was still missing. Though at least now he had proof she was alive.

"Did the woman happen to mention anything else?" Ruan prodded, hoping that perhaps Olive had been kind enough to furnish the man with her exact travel itinerary. It would save him a great deal of time if she had.

"She did not, though she did head off in the direction of the Quays. However that's not unusual, for there's not really anywhere else to go in Falmouth."

He laughed lightly at his own joke, only stopping when he saw the dark glare that Ruan cast him. There might be nowhere else to go in Falmouth bar the Quays, but from there a person could find passage to any corner of England, or the world for that matter.

"My thanks for your time." Ruan donned his hat, and pushed his way out the door onto Market Street. It bustled with a mixture of women, servants and sailors, all out shopping on the quaint cobblestone road. Ruan absently followed the tide of people, and soon found himself on Packet Quays. He tried to imagine himself in Olive's place, and how she would have viewed the chaotic docks. She had seemed nervous during her short time at the Port of Bristol, overwhelmed by the sheer noise and scale of the maritime activities. She would not have boarded a ship, he decided, especially not after what had happened on The Elizabeth. He turned to assess the nearby buildings, which mostly housed the offices of shipping merchants, and his eyes fell on a smaller building at the end of the row: A stage coach office.

Feeling certain that he would find some new information there, Ruan pushed his way through a group of navy men, freshly disembarked and eagerly searching for an inn to wet their newborn land legs. He crossed the road in a few long strides, dodging carriages and carts.

"I need some information on one of your recent passengers."

The clerk, who was seated at a tall wooden desk, blinked curiously at the formidable giant standing opposite him.

"You're going to have to be more specific," he replied mildly, glancing down at the papers on his desk. "I have nearly twenty coaches a day leaving here, and I'll be deuced if I can recall even one of the passengers. They all look the same, when you've been looking at them for a decade."

Another man, sitting on a long wooden bench, gave a snort of laughter at this remark.

"Aye, they all look the same," he agreed, taking a hearty sip of the pint of ale he was nursing. "And they all sound the same. Do you know what they sound like?"

Ruan shook his head.

"Annoying," the man supplied helpfully. "I wish I'd taken my Pa's advice and set up as a small farmer. Sheep don't moan and complain like passengers do."

"They rather smell, though, sheep," Ruan offered, as way of consoling the man for his poor career choice.

"And so do some of my passengers," this was delivered as a grunt. The clerk, sensing that his driver was about to lose him some business, hastily interrupted their exchange.

"Have you any specific details about this passenger you are seeking, sir?" he asked, pushing his spectacles up his nose, and looking at Ruan inquisitively. "Where they were heading? What day? Man, woman...or sheep?"

This brought a reluctant smile to Ruan's lips, and the driver choked on his ale with mirth.

"The passenger would have been a woman," Ruan leaned an elbow on the clerk's desk, "She would have travelled about two days ago. Red hair, green eyes, striking features."

The clerk frowned as he tried to recall if he had lately seen a beautiful red-head, he shook his head from side to side, indicating that the description meant nothing to him. Ruan had just begun to heave a sigh, when the driver spoke.

"Mayhaps it was the woman who went to St. Jarvis," the driver said, looking at his colleague, "The one who saved me from the lass with the spectacles. Remember her? She gave me a whole bloody history on the morals of the Romans, all the way from Truro to here. I thought she'd never stop yammerin', then the red head booked her passage and I foisted Miss Boring off onto her."

St. Jarvis, Ruan almost dropped dead at the name of the town. It was where he had spent most of his youth, as part of a marauding trio of hellions, which had consisted of him, Lord Deveraux and Lord Somerset. It was where he had met Catherine, where he had married her and, in the end, where he had buried her. He often thought of it as the last resting place of Ruan Ashford, for he had left it five years ago, to forever more be known as The Duke of Ruin.

"This woman," he spoke urgently, "Do you remember anything else about her? Did she give her name, or have many belongings? Did she say if she was staying in St. Jarvis or just passing through?"

The driver started at the intensity of Ruan's questioning. The Duke was a large man, his shoulders broader than most, and at six foot three he dwarfed both the driver and the clerk. His size was intimidating, which he mostly used to his advantage, but even when he was not trying to frighten or scare, the sheer mass of him did it anyway.

"She didn't say, sir," the driver held up his hands, as though Ruan had a weapon pointed at him. "She got off at St. Jarvis, and as far as I know she's still there. There's only one coach that services the town, and that's mine. I haven't seen her since I left her, so you can deduce from that what you will."

Ruan took a calming breath, and tried to quell the restless urgency that had begun to hum in his very bones. He needed to get to St. Jarvis, and now, but he had other matters to attend to before he left Falmouth.

"My thanks, gentlemen," he said, pivoting on the heel of his Hessian to leave. He knew that behind his back the two men would be exchanging shocked glances, or perhaps mouthing obscenities to each other, but he didn't care. He now knew where Olive was, and that was all that mattered.

"Black," he called once he reached the inn, banging furiously on the door to the Captain's room. The Captain opened the door quickly, his face surprised by the ferocity of the Duke's hammering.

"Your Grace," he said, his face confused. He was half dressed, in simple breeches and a white shirt, undone to reveal a glimpse of his chest. Ruan was just about to accuse him of being bone idle, when he caught sight of the Captain's desk over his shoulder. It was covered in maps, letters and important looking documents.

"I have been corresponding with your man of business in Bristol, and the insurance company," Black said by way of explanation for the mess. He invited the Duke to come in, with a simple gesture of his hand. Ruan saw that the room, apart from the desk, was spotless. The bed was made to navy standards, the Captain's boots stood polished by the doorway, as though waiting inspection.

"I think I know where her Grace has gone," he said shortly, standing before the fireplace, despite the fact that the grate was empty. June, like May before it, had brought relentlessly hot weather, punctuated only by the occasional storm attempting to break the heat.

"Wonderful," Black beamed, genuinely glad, it seemed, of the news. He had been sending men daily to search the coastline, near where The Elizabeth had gone down, despite Ruan's protests that his wife was alive. All the Captain's searches had turned up was Olive's portmanteau, battered and a little sodden, but still whole.

"I'll be leaving in the next hour," Ruan continued, but was cut off by the sudden arrival of a breathless cabin boy.

"Beg pardon Captain," the boy rushed, then caught a glimpse of the Duke, "Oh sorry, your Grace I did not know you were here."

The young boy was struck dumb at the sight of the Duke, and Black had to prod him to share what had brought him there in the first place.

"There's a messenger from Southampton, Captain," the boy said nervously, "He says that the tar you think blew up The Elizabeth is being held at the Port. He was caught trying to board a ship to France."

The Captain glanced at Ruan speculatively.

"Is this something you wish me to deal with, your Grace?"

"No," Ruan shook his head slowly; he didn't want anyone else dealing with the villain, bar him. He had plans aplenty for the cur, plans which included running him through with a sword, or flaying him alive with a whip.

"But, the Duchess?"

"I'll look after that," Ruan brushed away his Captain's concerns. He still had a few friends in Cornwall, and he could think of one who would be perfect for keeping an eye on his runaway bride until he returned.

"Find my valet," Ruan instructed the young cabin boy, "Have him ready the horses. Black meet me outside in half an hour, I'll want you there to help identify the man...and to hold me back in case I try to strangle the blighter before he tells me who hired him."

Ruan stalked from the Captain's room to his own; he needed to pen a quick letter before he left, with instructions to his friend to not let Olive out of their sight until he returned. And then —he smiled— then he would take his errant wife over his knee if he had to, to convince her to come home.

What a difference a fortnight could make. Liv, Jane and Sally the housemaid seconded from Jarvis House, had spent two weeks furiously scrubbing, cleaning and dusting the boarding house so that it sparkled. They had polished the sweeping staircase in the entrance hall, so that the mahogany wood took on a warm, reddish shine. They had dusted the cobwebs from the library, and when they moved the settee inside, Liv could actually envision the saloons being held there. And then, when the beds in all the rooms were dressed with fresh linen, the guests began to trickle in.

The first to arrive were the Hamerstone twins, Miss Poppy and Miss Alexandra. Identical down to their very toes, they were a high-spirited pair, and Liv adored them from the off.

"Gemini!" Poppy exclaimed, as they were ushered through the door. "It looks just the same as it did in Mrs Baker's days."

"Only better," Alexandra interjected as she beamed at Olive, and dropped her bags on the rug,before twirling around and bouncing with excitement. The twins were trailed by their aunt Augusta Hamerstone, who looked exhausted after the long coach journey. Olive couldn't blame her; if this was what the twins were like after three days ensconced inside a cramped carriage, then she was sure they'd be twice as sprightly when well rested.

"You're the first guests to arrive," Olive explained, as she led the trio upstairs to their suite of rooms. "We're expecting a full house by week's end."

And indeed by the time Saturday evening arrived, the boarding house had a no vacancies sign hung outside its door. The other guests were an eclectic mix of authors, historians, musicians and philosophers. Most were ladies who elsewhere would have been dubbed spinsters, but in St. Jarvis found sanctuary from society's labels. The only man amongst their ranks was a Mr Alastair Jackson, a very serious young fellow of thirty, who wore spectacles which magnified his eyes and gave him the appearance of a startled bug. Which was quite apt, as Mr. Jackson was involved in the business of entomology, which a rather flustered Jane explained was the study of insects.

"He's a genius," she whispered to Olive, as she helped her prepare tea in the kitchen. Jane's face was beet red, as it was wont to turn when she was discussing Mr. Jackson, and she wore the look of an excited puppy. Her movements were jerky, and as she made to pour milk into the small serving jug, she spilled the pail all over the flagstone floor.

"Oh, no!" Jane exclaimed, hopping out of the way of the encroaching puddle of milk, "Look how stupid I am."

Her face, already pink, was wreathed in dismay. Tears welled up in her eyes, visible even behind her glasses, and Liv gave her a comforting pat on the elbow.

"There's no use fretting over shed milk," Liv gently consoled her, dropping a dishcloth to the floor and wiping it on the puddle with the toe of her boot. "No harm done to either of us, or your pretty slippers, and that's the most important thing!"

"But there'll be none for breakfast," Jane wailed, wringing her hands in despair. It was true, the pail which held the milk for the breakfast was now empty, its contents having been completely emptied onto the floor, but Liv shrugged lightly.

"I'll just bring the trays into the library," she said evenly, lifting a heavy tray up easily, "And then I shall run down to Mr. Lawless at the tavern, he's bound to lend me a jug until tomorrow."

"Oh, no let me," Jane protested passionately, "If you go, you'll miss Mr. Jackson's lecture on the Hemipetra species of insects he's been studying at the cove."

"Oh, drat," Liv struggled to sound genuinely remorseful in response to her friend's scholarly enthusiasm. "You stay Jane, then you can relay back to me what he says, you've a far better memory than I."

Liv said this very firmly, and there was a grain of truth in her statement. Jane would remember Mr. Jackson's lecture far better than Liv would, for Jane would avidly hang on the entomologist's every word, whereas Liv would struggle to keep her eyes open. Let alone her ears.

Firmly she prodded her friend into the library and set about serving the tea to her guests, before discreetly excusing herself to fetch the milk.

The boarding house was situated at the top of the steep hill on which St. Jarvis was built. The village was made up of one main street, comprising of quaint houses and shops all leaning against each other. The steep road wound down to a small cove, where a few small fishing boats were moored. Liv pulled her shawl tightly around herself, to ward off the cool evening's breeze, as she scurried toward The Fisherman's Friend, the one and only tavern in the tiny village.

She welcomed the break that the walk granted her, for the past few days had been frantic, filled with serving her guests, as well as attending to the cleaning of their rooms. Liv rose at dawn and did not go to bed again until all her guests had retired for the night. She needed more help; Jane was good to her, but unused to domestic activities, and quite scatterbrained despite her obvious intelligence.

"Here she is," Mr Lawless called as Liv pushed open the stiff, saltwater-swollen door of The Fisherman's Friend. A group of weather beaten fishermen were perched on stools at the long bar, which took up most of the space in the tiny tavern.

"Mrs Black," they mumbled in unison, raising their tankards in greeting to her. Liv rather enjoyed her status as a widow. In Frome she had always been the daughter of the local Lord, and the villagers — while outwardly deferential — had never sought her friendship, or aired their honest opinions. In St. Jarvis, however, she had found the local population more than friendly, eager to take her under their wing.

"Gentlemen," she said with a stiff nod of greeting, befitting of a widow, "I hope the evening finds you well."

"It's much brighter now that you're here," Mr Lawless beamed, throwing the dishrag in his hands over his shoulder. "What can I do for you Mrs Black? A pint of bitter?"

"No,thank you." Liv gave a self conscious smile, " I wondered if I could borrow a pail of milk until tomorrow?"

"Anything for you m'dear," Mr Lawless said with a saucy wink that left Liv rather red-faced. The proprietor of the tavern was seventy if he was a day, but his rheumy blue eyes still twinkled mischievously. He disappeared through a low door, which led to his private rooms, leaving Liv standing awkwardly in the dim tavern.

"So you're the widow Black, that I've heard so much about."

The voice that spoke was accented with money and privilege, though there was a definite slur to the words. Liv whirled around, and saw who it was that had addressed her. A man, of about her father's age, who was seated alone by the hearth, clearly in his cups. His clothes were fine as any Lord's, and Liv knew for certain that she was looking at a member of the ton.

"I am," she replied steadily, her voice carrying across the room. She would not walk to him; let him say what he had to say for everyone to hear. "Though we have not been introduced, sir, so I do not know your name."

"Keyford," the man grunted, standing to his feet and swaying unsteadily. "I am Lord Keyford, of Aylesbury. And you my dear are not welcome in this town. Trying to dreg up old ghosts, eh? Well St. Jarvis has been peaceful since that old bat died and the boarding house closed. I won't have it, I won't have you here."

Lord Keyford lunged for Olive, who was so taken aback by his outburst that she was momentarily paralysed with shock. It was only the quick intervention of another customer, a black haired woman who had been dining alone, that saved her.

"Oops a daisy," the woman sang, in a broad Northern accent, as she stood and grabbed Lord Keyford by the elbow. "I think you've had a bit too much to drink, my Lord."

Her voice was firm, and Liv could see that her grip on Keyford's elbow was even firmer. The drunken Lord raised two, thick, grey eyebrows in confusion, as he struggled to register that he was being frogmarched to the door.

"I want to have a word with the Widow Black," he protested, but his captor simply smiled sweetly at him as she blatantly ignored his protests.

"And you shall, my Lord," the dark haired woman crooned, as she opened the creaking door, "But just not tonight."

Olive watched, open mouthed, as the woman gave Lord Keyford a gentle, but firm, push out the door and slammed it in his wake. She stared with satisfaction at the closed door for a moment, before turning to the elderly fishermen, still sat at the bar.

"Fat lot of help you lot were," the dark haired woman grumbled at them.

"I can't bite the hand that feeds me, lass," one of the older men defended himself, glancing apologetically at Olive as he spoke. "Lord Keyford is my landlord, if I'd manhandled him the way you had, I'd be sleeping under a bush tonight."

"Aye," the other men choroused in agreement, staring down at their pints of ale and avoiding Olive's eye.

"I am most grateful," Olive ventured to the woman, "If there's anything that I can do for you, please allow me."

"You're Mrs Black?"

The question was delivered in that abrupt, no-nonsense, Northern accent that brokered no arguments or lies. Olive nodded, her eyes locking with the woman's own, which were a troubled shade of grey.

"And you run the boarding house," the woman continued, still watching her closely with unreadable eyes.

Again Olive nodded, wondering if perhaps this fierce Northerner was going to request a bed for the night.

"I'm Polly," the woman stuck out her hand for Olive to shake, "Polly Jenkins. I'm looking for work around these parts Mrs Black, and I heard you might be looking."

"Oh,' Olive was momentarily taken aback by the directness of Polly's statement. She hadn't expected to find her new maid in a tavern, but the woman looked capable and strong, and Olive liked the straightness of her character.

"I'd be delighted to take you on, Mrs Jenkins," Liv replied, a warm smile creasing her face, for she would be glad to have this Polly Jenkins on her side. Though small in stature, Polly looked strong, and she radiated energy.

"Did I miss something?"

Mr Lawless was back, a pail of milk in his hands, and a look of bemusement on his lined face as he regarded the silent men at the bar, who were avidly watching the exchange between Mrs Black and Polly.

"Only the local lord being escorted out, on account of his rudeness to Mrs Black," Polly replied demurely.

"Old Keyford was in his cups, I should have cut him off after the last pint," Lawless glanced at Liv, his eyes full of apologies. "He's only recently back from Southampton, he always drinks like a fish when he's back from there. And to add to it, he's probably drowning his sorrows, now he's heard that his son in law survived the downing of The Elizabeth."

Olive bit back a gasp — Lord Keyford was the father of her husband's late wife. He had seemed bitter, and now she knew why; to outlive your child was every parent's worst nightmare.

"I'm sure Lord Keyford will be filled with remorse on the morrow," Liv said lightly, not believing for a minute that the old man would. She did not wish to stand and talk about the drunken Lord, however, for now that she knew who he was she felt a stab of pity for him.

"Thank you for the milk, Mr Lawless," she said, with a bright smile, relieving the man of the pail he held. "I will replace it tomorrow."

"Goodnight, Mrs Black," Lawless said with a gap toothed grin, and the men at the bar echoed him. Liv waited for Polly to fetch her bag from the table, and settle up with Lawless for her supper. When she was quite ready Liv led her out onto the quiet road.

There was not a sinner to be seen as the pair made their way up the steep hill toward the boarding house, watched only by the silent houses of the village.

"Have you been in St. Jarvis for long?" Liv ventured as they walked.

"Only arrived this evening," Polly said in reply, her grey eyes scanning the buildings as they strolled past.

"And what brought you so far south?" Liv asked, wondering how such a lively creature had ended up in such a remote part of Cornwall. Polly did not seem like a woman who wished to while away her life in a sleepy backwater like St. Jarvis.

"My husband passed," Polly avoided Liv's eye, instead focusing on the road ahead. "He was a sailor and he left me widowed in Bristol, but the city's no place for a woman alone."

"You're right, it's no place for a widow."

As she spoke Liv glanced down at her companion's right hand. There was no ring there, though when Polly saw where Liv's eyes rested, she arched an eyebrow and looked pointedly at Liv's own bare ring finger.

"Did you love him, Mrs Black?" Polly asked quietly, as they neared the boarding house. "Your husband, I mean."

Liv pondered the question for a moment; perhaps it was a normal exchange between women who had lost their husbands, but it unsettled her a little.

"I barely knew him," she finally answered, for it was the truth.

Ruan's hand was itching to form itself into a fist, and thoroughly punch the recalcitrant man seated before him. They were in the small, damp gaol near the docks, where George Beattie — the tar who had blown up The Elizabeth — was being held. Ruan had been informed that Beattie hailed from Bristol, and was a well known thief, who often acted as hired muscle for local criminal gangs.

"I'll ask you one more time," Ruan said, in a voice so low and menacing that even the magistrate who had accompanied him to Beattie's cell, quaked upon hearing it. "Who paid you to wreck The Elizabeth?"

"And I told you," Beattie sneered, "I don't bloody well know."

Whack.

Ruan delivered a blow so forceful to the sailor's chin, that he fell from his chair to the floor.

"Are you going to let him punch me like that?"

"Punch you like what?" the magistrate replied blandly, to Beattie's outraged protests. "I didn't see a thing."

Ruan suppressed a grin; if he was so inclined he could have strangled Beattie to death and the magistrate wouldn't have blinked an eyelid. Such was the power of his title. But Ruan wasn't there to kill Beattie, he didn't need to for he would surly hang on the gallows for his crime; Ruan just wanted to know who had paid him to commit the act in the first place.

"Once again Mr Beattie," he said softly, advancing on the young man, who was still sprawled on the cold, hard ground of the gaol cell. "Who paid you to wreck The Elizabeth?"

"I don't know."

This time Beattie sounded scared, as he made his reply, his eyes darting around the cell, as though searching for a means of escape. "If I knew I'd tell you, but it was dark when I met him. Alls I know is that he sounded like a toff. He spoke just like you did, your Grace."

Ruan frowned; this information didn't narrow down his list of suspects by many. Every aristocratic male of the ton spoke with the same clipped vowels; the product of an Eton education.

"Where did you meet with this man?" he asked.

"The alley behind The Seven Stars, in Redcliff, your Grace," the prisoner offered reluctantly. "I was relieving myself after a couple of pints, and he approached me from behind."

"Brave man, to approach a man engaged in that particular act."

Beattie snorted with laughter; "Aye, he was, but he came ready with a bag of coins the weight of a small calf, and the promise of another once the act was done."

"And you were to collect the second payment here, in Southampton?"

"Aye," Beattie grimaced, "And then I was to take a boat to France and disappear."

"You'll disappear alright, young man," the magistrate interjected, "In a few weeks time you'll hang for this, and the world will forget that George Beattie ever existed."

At these bleak words, the young man paled, and Ruan knew that he would get no more answers from him. Still, he ventured to ask one final question.

"When were you supposed to have met this gentleman, Mr Beattie?"

"Last night, your Grace," the criminal replied.

Damn; so whoever it was that had hired Beattie, would already have heard of his incarceration and fled. Ruan thanked the magistrate for his time, and left the gaol to return to the coaching inn. Southampton had been a clever choice for a meeting place, Ruan decided. The town had a port that was moderately busy due to the Navy ships which docked there, but was also highly fashionable with the gentry. They came from London to take the waters at the spa, and as Ruan walked through the bustling city streets toward his hotel, he spotted a familiar face.

"Lavelle," he called, much surprised to see his friend hurrying in the direction of the port.

"Everleigh," Henry Lavelle, Lord Somerset turned at the sound of his name, and a wide grin broke across his handsome face. "I've been looking for you, heard from your Captain Black that you'd been down to the gaol to interview the cur who blew up The Elizabeth."

"Aye, I did," Ruan grimaced, "Though fat lot of help he was. What brings you all the way down here?"

"Why, you of course; it's all over London that someone tried to kill you. You can't blame your second for hot footing it down, in case you needed my services."

Ruan tried not to wince at the innocuous reference to duelling; Henry had once acted as his second in the first, and only, duel that Ruan had ever partaken in. He had been there to witness Ruan shooting dead Charles Birmingham, the man who had been having an affair with his late wife. Though contrary to rumour, Ruan had only killed the blighter because Birmingham had turned before the count, and shot Ruan in the leg. The man had been deranged, and for what he had done to Catherine, Ruan felt little regret for having taken his life.

"Are you staying in The Dolphin?"

"Where else?" Ruan replied, as Lavelle fell into step beside him. The Dolphin Hotel was England's largest and grandest coaching inn, and after the long journey from Falmouth, Ruan wouldn't countenance staying anywhere that wasn't the height of luxury.

The men repaired to the hotel saloon, and over brandy Ruan shared with Lavelle his suspicions that someone was trying to kill him, the story of how The Elizabeth had sank, as well as Olive's disappearance.

"Any idea where she is?"

For the first time in Lavelle's life, he seemed to be struggling to speak. His face was pale and drawn, it seemed he was shocked to his very core. Ruan felt touched by his obvious worry, though said nothing. Speaking about feelings wasn't the done thing, for men of their ilk.

"Actually," he said, taking a deep sip of his brandy, "I know exactly where she is, and you do too."

"I do?"

"St. Jarvis," Ruan supplied, and he was gratified to see Lavelle splutter on the drink he had taken.

"Good Lord," the blonde haired man gasped, as he struggled to regain his composure. "I haven't been there in years. Not since — not since —"

Catherine's death; though in truth Lavelle hadn't spent that much time in St. Jarvis at all past the age of eighteen. Once he had inherited, he had moved to London to engage in debauchery on a grander scale, and forgotten clean about the small seaside village. Ruan could see the wistful look in his friend's eyes, as he thought on the place they had spent so many of their youthful summers.

"Is that where you're headed now?" Lavelle asked, his expression thoughtful.

"Aye, it is — and if you'd like to join me, you'd be more than welcome. I think I might need my second, if Lord Keyford spies me there."

His late wife's father despised him, and with good reason, for he thought Ruan responsible for his daughter's death. The Duke knew for certain that if he saw him, Keyford was liable to do anything, such was the venom he held for Ruan.

"Good God," Lavelle put down his glass. "Keyford has an estate nearby, do you remember Catherine used to say he spent half his time down this way?"

Ruan had, and the same suspicions had crossed his mind. Keyford held a small estate in Nursling, and half the world knew that this was where he had housed his mistress, and his illegitimate offspring. It had been a bone of contention between Catherine and her father; another thing to argue about in a family that had made hurt and anger into an art form.

"We'll deal with Keyford, when we see him," Ruan finally said, a note of regret to his tone. The ghosts of his past kept resurfacing, and it seemed that to claim his future with Olive, he would have to confront them all.

The next day Olive awoke to the scent of baking bread, wafting from the kitchen below her. She washed and dressed quickly, ashamed that she had slept so late, when she had guests to feed and serve.

"You find your way about very quickly," she said with surprise to Polly, who had the entire table set, as well as fresh bread made, and sausages, rashers and pudding frying in a pan on the hob.

"If you can find your way around one kitchen, then you can find your way around them all," the young woman said cheerily, with a smile on her face, which was slightly red from the heat of the oven and the steam rising from the various pots.

"Let me help you," Liv said, reaching for an apron so that she could muck in with the cooking.

"Oh, no m'am," the other woman shook her head stubbornly, "That's what I'm here for, the grunt work. You shouldn't be serving meals, not when you're the proprietor."

"But I've been serving the guests since their arrival," Olive replied with a laugh, "They'll think me bone idle if I suddenly sit down at the table."

But Polly was not to be deterred, and so Olive took her place at the head of the table, as breakfast was served to her guests. They arrived in dribs and drabs; the Hamerstone twins were the first to sit down, both girls in high spirits as was usual.

"A Lady must never offer too many opinions in public, Poppy" the twin's beleaguered Aunt Augusta said, closing her eyes as though in pain, as Poppy entered into a heated debate with Mr Jackson on the merits of daily exercise for ladies.

"But you've never had an opinion you didn't care to share, Aunt," Alexandra replied innocently,coming to the rescue of her twin, to which Augusta scowled.

Olive bit back a smile; it wouldn't do to be seen taking sides. Instead she engaged Augusta in mild conversation about local gossip, while Poppy continued to argue with Mr. Jackson. Olive kept half an ear on what was passing between the two; it seemed Mr. Jackson had strong beliefs on what a woman should do in her spare time — and exercising wasn't one of the activities he deemed acceptable. On his list of preferred activities for young ladies were reading, sewing, painting, dancing...Olive stifled a yawn. She hadn't expected a man who had been so enthusiastic about the boarding house reopening to be so stiff and rigid in his beliefs.

Mercifully Mr. Jackson soon excused himself for a morning of scouring the coves for water-born insects. As he left the room, Olive saw Poppy stick her tongue out at his retreating back, though luckily Augusta missed this very unladylike act.

The other guests arrived down after the twins and their harassed Aunt had left for a day of walking the impressive cliffs around St. Jarvis. Audrey Dunham, the willowy poetess amongst their ranks, sipped at black tea absently while Petronella Devoy, the daughter of a Viscount, happily ate everything that was set before her. The two had been friends for years, they explained to Olive, and had spent many summers at Mrs Bakers', where the freedom St. Jarvis granted gave them time to pursue their literary inclinations.

"And what do you write, Miss Devoy?" Olive asked, casually, though once she brokered the question the two women exchanged rather furtive glances.

"Pamphlets mostly," Petronella said in a whisper, her eyes on the door lest anyone walk in on their conversation. "They're of a rather political persuasion."

Gracious; Olive tried not to look too alarmed. She hadn't known she was housing political activists under her own roof. Petronella was beautiful and titled, and probably could have her pick of any man of the ton — even though she was now miles past marriageable age. Olive had to admire her bravery and her convictions; she was certain that Viscount Devoy did not approve of his daughter's interests.

The final guests to take breakfast were Mrs Actrol, an author who had been close to the late Mrs Baker, and her travelling companion Beatrice, who seemed to exist only to do Mrs Actrol's bidding. Both women chatted politely to Olive, expressing their happiness that she had now found help for the domestic tasks.

"You can take your place at the head of the table," Mrs Actrol sniffed, "And stop that flibbertigibbet Mr Jackson monopolising all conversation." Beatrice nodded furiously, her soft, mousy face crossed with an expression of disdain at the mention of the in-house entomologist.

"Oh, dear," Liv put down her tea cup, "I hadn't realised he was upsetting you Mrs Actrol."

"Upsetting me?"

The older woman drew herself up imperiously,casting Liv a rather disdainful look.

"I have lived through several wars, young lady," she said evenly, "Pursued a career that many thought scandalous. I have dined with kings and thieves, and traveled the continent alone. That dullard Mr Jackson could no more upset me than you could. He bores me, nothing more, nothing less. But I do hate to be bored. Especially by men who think that by speaking to you, they are bestowing on you a great favour."

Beatrice, Liv decided, was just short of banging the table, her approval of Mrs Actrol's speech was so great.

"Flibbertigibbet," the mousy lady whispered instead, her lips pursed in disapproval. Both women departed soon after, for a boating trip around the cove, leaving Liv to ruminate on what they had told her.

"You were right," she said later to Polly, as they were stripping the linen from the beds. "I do need to be present at meal times."

The other woman smiled, but said nothing, and continued folding the sheets. They were on the final room, having worked quickly as a team. Polly had initially protested when Liv had offered to assist her, but she had put her foot down. She had to do some of the work.

Outside the open door, there was the sound of footsteps scurrying up the stairs. Whoever was approaching seemed in a desperate hurry.

"Olive, there you are!"

It was Jane, her cheeks rosy and pink from the exertion of her climb. "I'm sorry I couldn't come sooner, but Julian has a guest arriving to stay, and he insisted I was there to greet him. I —oh—hello."

Jane paused, as she caught sight of Polly, her face curious.

"Jane this is Polly Jenkins," Liv made the introduction, for they had not met the night before. "Polly this is Miss Jane Deveraux, my good friend and sister to Lord Deveraux."

"Don't hold the last fact against me," Jane quipped, with a bright smile to Polly, who seemed nervous about being introduced to one of the gentry. "When did you arrive? This is marvelous, I've been telling Olive that she needs some proper help."

As she and Polly finished dressing the bed, Olive relayed the story of Lord Keyford's dreadful behaviour at the inn, and how Polly had come to her rescue.

"Oh dear," Jane chewed on her lip, as she took in all that had been said. "It is abominable behaviour on Lord Keyford's part, but —"

Olive watched Jane carefully; a cascade of emotions were passing across her face. Sadness, fear, anger, as she thought on the belligerent Lord. "But what?" she gently prompted, and Jane blinked.

"Lord Keyford is the father of the late Duchess of Everleigh," Jane whispered, as though afraid someone might overhear them. "Catherine was close to my brother growing up, but she was even closer to Mrs Baker, for she loved to read and daydream."

Olive nodded, not wishing to say anything lest she interrupt Jane's reverie. She was more than a little curious to know about the late Catherine Ashford, and with a quick glance at Polly, she saw a similar interest in the other woman's eyes. She thought nothing of it, for the story of Catherine's demise had made the papers, and was known the length and breadth of the country. What Olive wanted to know, was if Ruan had spoken the truth when he told her that he had not killed his wife.

"Catherine was beautiful, but impetuous," Jane continued, sadly, "She was given over to great mood swings, and her father blamed Mrs Baker. He said she had corrupted his daughter with libertine ideas — but he was wrong. Catherine was happiest here. She had such a wonderful mind, but when it wasn't being stimulated, she became bored, angry, even reckless. She was not well, I think, not well at all."

Jane paused, looking at the two women who were watching her, avidly hanging on her every word.

"All this," she whispered, nervously, "Is of course highly confidential. Poor Catherine was a troubled soul, I should not have gossiped about her so."

"You're not gossipping," Polly spoke firmly but kindly, "You're merely informing Mrs Black of why she should be cautious around Lord Keyford."

Olive started at the mention of her name, for her mind had wandered. She had not known anything about the late Duchess, and what she had learnt now left her confused.

"You said," Olive ventured,wondering if she was overstepping a line, but not caring in her urgency to know. "The first day that we met, that you didn't think that the Duke had killed his wife."

"I don't," Jane shook her head fiercely, as though to banish the very idea from the room. "I knew Everleigh as a boy, and he was kind. He married Catherine because he loved her, he would never have hurt her. It was an accident, I swear it."

The room was silent for a moment, as the three women thought on the tragic fate of Catherine Ashford. Liv felt a momentary pang of regret for Ruan, who had been castigated by society for a murder he apparently had not committed. Though he had killed Catherine's lover, that much was true.

"Well," Liv brushed down the front of her dress, and said the only thing she could think of. "How about a cup of tea?"

The ladies trooped down the stairs to the kitchen, where Liv set about boiling water for their well deserved libations. Jane had manoeuvred the conversation from the morbid to her favourite topic: Mr. Jackson.

"He simply has the most marvellous brain," she was enthusiastically telling Polly, who looked rather unimpressed. "You should see his collection of preserved larvae, simply fascinating to view."

"I'll take your word for it," Polly looked rather green around the gills at the thought of a case full of dead insects. "Is he very romantic?" she asked, accepting a cup of steaming tea from Liv, who joined them at the table. "Your Mr. Jackson? Does he read you poems and the like?"

"He's not my Mr. Jackson," Jane protested, but Polly simply guffawed in disbelief. Shyly Jane gave both women a tremulous smile, and lowered her voice as she began to speak.

"Though, actually," she whispered, her ears turning red, "Even though he's not mine just yet, he has asked me to meet with him here, this evening. He says he has most important business to discuss."

"Cor."

This was from Polly, whose Northern accent was more pronounced when she was excited. Liv felt a strange stab of nerves for Jane, who looked so hopeful. She was no longer sure what she thought of this Mr. Jackson, now that she had heard him pontificate to the twins, and Mrs Actrol's damning opinion of him. Perhaps he was too stuffy for Jane, who though bookish and outwardly meek, was at heart a romantic.

"I hope whatever he's proposing is in your best interests Jane," she cautioned,

"I hope he proposes," Polly interjected, with a giggle, which left Jane even more red-faced.

"Oh, hush," she whispered, glancing at the kitchen door as though she feared Mr. Jackson was outside listening. "What Mr. Jackson and I share is a mutual love of the academics. I couldn't hope that a man of his ilk would even deign to consider marrying me."

"But you're the daughter of a Viscount, and pretty as a peach!"

Jane started at Polly's indignant outburst, though she looked terribly pleased to have been called pretty. She was, in fact, very pretty; with soft, alabaster skin like fresh snow and huge amber eyes behind her spectacles. It was a wonder no one had ever told her before.

"Oh," she brushed away Polly's compliment. "I'm not. Julian says I'm as pale as a ghost from staying indoors reading, and that no man would ever love a woman as bookish as I."

"Who's this Julian then?" Polly snorted, "He sounds like a right prig."

"My brother."

There was an awkward silence, in which Liv felt herself seething with anger at the bullying Lord Deveraux while Polly frowned.

"Don't listen to a word he says, Jane," she consoled her friend, reaching across the table and patting her hand.

"Oh I'd love to have to never listen to a word he says again," Jane pasted a brave smile on her face, and stood up, "But, alas, I must attend luncheon back at the house with him. For Lord Payne is visiting and I have been summoned to the table."

Olive blinked; she recognised that name from her season in town. Lord Payne was next in line to the ducal seat of Hawkfield, though until he came into his title, he seemed content to merely entertain the ton with his outrageous hi-jinx. The papers had recently been filled with tales of a phaeton race he had orchestrated on Rotten Row, which had ended with him being thrown bodily into a fountain, and his expensive new vehicle smashed to smithereens.

"I can see you've heard of him," Jane noted Liv's raised eyebrows with a wry smile, "Just thank goodness that you don't have to dine with him." With that she was gone, with promises to return later that evening. Polly and Liv were silent for a few minutes after she left, each sipping thoughtfully on their tea.

"Well," Polly finally spoke, setting her cup down firmly. "It seems St. Jarvis is the Cornish outpost for the whole of the ton, from what I've gathered this morning. Dukes, Viscounts — I wouldn't be surprised if the Prince himself appears."

"Nor I," Liv gave a faint laugh; Prince George she could deal with; the only member of the aristocracy that she didn't want to show up in the little village was the Duke of Everleigh.

"Good Lord, Everleigh, it's been years!"

Julian Deveraux, Viscount Jarvis, greeted his old friend with a resounding clap to the back, that was so enthusiastic it nearly sent Ruan flying across the marble entrance hall of Jarvis House.

"Haven't seen you since—ah—ah—"

"It's been a long time," Ruan smiled tightly. He and Jarvis hadn't crossed paths since Catherine's funeral; not out of intention, but their ways had simply parted. Jarvis spent most of his time in town, falling out of gentleman's clubs at dawn, whilst Ruan had resolutely avoided such establishments.

"I'm told you have company," he said, as the Viscount led him into the elegantly appointed drawing room, where Jane, Deveraux's sister sat. Her face was pained, as the man opposite her spoke, gesticulating wildly, a grin as wide as the Avon Gorge across his handsome face.

"Payne," Deveraux called, and the young buck stopped mid-sentence to look up at his friend. "Have you met Everleigh?"

Lord Payne stood to greet the Duke, his hand outstretched. "Can't say I've had the pleasure, though I've heard of you, of course."

"Of course," Everleigh took the young man's hand, in a firm grip. "And I you. Your altercation with a fountain was all the papers could talk about for weeks."

"Oh, that," Lord Payne ruffled his hair with his hand, so that it fell in the same dishevelled manner that Byron had made so popular. "I was just telling Jane all about it. Riveting stuff."

"Truly riveting," the young woman echoed, though her tone was less than impressed. When her eyes fell on Ruan however, they lit up with warmth. She stood, and took his hand in hers, giving a squeeze to convey her happiness. "Everleigh, it's so lovely to see you again. I have missed you so."

"You do me a great honour, Jane," he said, bestowing a genuine smile on her. "Tell me, what have you been up to since we last spoke?"

"Oh," Jane blinked, and earnestly pushed her glasses up her nose. "I've been writing an essay on the morality of the Romans. It's quite fascinating, I—"

"Everleigh was just being polite," Julian drawled, rudely interrupting his sister mid-speech. "He doesn't actually care what boring bit of history you've decided to resurrect."

Ruan watched Jane's face flood with embarrassment, and the urge to strike Lord Deveraux filled him. Julian had always shown disdain for Jane, when they were younger, but Ruan had thought it merely the natural emotion that a teenage boy would feel for his younger sibling. Ruan, himself an only child, had always envied Julian his adoring little sister, but the pompous git had never appreciated her. It seemed he still didn't, even all these years later.

"I should be most grateful to receive a copy of the essay, when it's done," he said pointedly to Jane, ignoring Lord Deveraux who was rolling his eyes. "I always find your work fascinating, Jane."

Jane blinked at him shyly, the tips of her ears going red. She cast a glance at her brother, and Lord Payne, who looked bored beyond belief, then smiled at Ruan.

"I must leave now, your Grace," she said brightly, the relief at not having to suffer any more of her brother's company evident on her face. "Will you be here when I return?"

"I'm afraid not, I was merely stopping on my way to Pemberton Hall. I have been travelling from Southampton these past few days."

"But you will be staying in Cornwall, your Grace?"

Ruan hesitated; he had no idea what he would do, once he had Olive back under his protection. Pemberton, his Cornish estate, was much smaller than the Ducal seat he held in Avon, but perhaps it would be a nice spot to acquaint himself better with his wife.

"I do not know," he answered honestly, "But if I stay, I will call again."

Mollified Jane fled the room, with the briefest of nods to her brother and no acknowledgement to Lord Payne, who didn't seem to notice the slight for he was checking his hair in the looking glass above the fireplace.

"How about a brandy?" Lord Deveraux cried, rubbing his hands together with anticipation. It was rather early in the afternoon for drinking, but after the long journey from Southampton, Ruan felt he deserved some steeling libations.

He followed Deveraux and Payne to the mahogany clad library, where a low fire burned in the imposing hearth, despite the warmth of the summer's day. Both men seemed well acquainted with the room; Payne threw himself into a cosy, stuffed chair, with the air of a man who was familiar with the action.

"What brings you to St.Jarvis?" Ruan asked the younger man, as he accepted a tumbler from Deveraux. He had poured Ruan a rather generous measure, and an even more generous one for himself.

Lord Payne grimaced, as though he was in pain, and cast Ruan a dejected look.

"Trying to out-run my father's ire."

Ruan snorted into his brandy. He knew the Duke of Hawkfield well from Parliamentary sessions, and he was a fierce, proud man. That his son had garnered a reputation as the ton's most committed reprobate, would not sit well the old Duke.

"I don't blame you," Ruan sipped on his drink, "The old man even scares me."

Hearing that the fearsome Duke of Ruin found his father intimidating seemed to mollify Payne somewhat.

"He'll be even more eager to find me a bride, now," Payne said dejectedly, then a thought seemed to strike him. "I say, Everleigh, did you find your missing wife? Is that why you're back in Cornwall?"

No one would ever accuse Lord Payne of an excess of social tact, Ruan thought with a grimace.

"Nearly," he said, "I have reason to believe that after The Elizabeth sank, that she somehow ended up in St. Jarvis."

"Good God," Deveraux had paled, and was looking at Ruan nervously. "Did she lose her mind, do you think, from the shock of it all?"

Ruan could read the expression of pity on his old friend's face. Not another mad wife, he could see Deveraux thinking. He shrugged, in answer to the question, and took another sip of his drink.

"I wonder where she's staying," th Viscount mused aloud, after a moment's thoughtful silence. "A widow named Mrs Black recently reopened the old boarding house, and it's full of eccentrics like the old days. Perhaps she's there?"

"Mrs Black?" Ruan raised his eyebrows speculatively.

"Yes, Olive Black. A sailor's widow. She has quite the sharp tongue, but one lets that slide on account of how pretty she is. I was always partial to a red head though..."

"Gentlemen," Ruan set his glass down on the small table beside his chair. "I think you might find that I am the Widow Black's husband, and rumours of my death have been greatly exaggerated."

That evening the boarding house was filled with the sound of music and laughter, as the twins gave an impromptu musicale in the drawing room. Poppy played the piano forte, whilst Alexandra accompanied her on the harp. Both girls sang, with sweet clear voices, that quite often faltered, as they both descended into fits of giggles. The music had begun sedately, but once their Aunt Augusta had retired for the night, the twins had unveiled their secret talent for bawdy tunes, more suited to a tavern than a group of ladies —though no one complained.

Olive kept half an ear on the twins' songs, as she prepared a tray of tea in the kitchen. She was torn between asking them to stop, before things got too rowdy and Augusta was disturbed, and genuinely enjoying the innuendo laden ditties. As she filled the China pot with boiling water, she heard a movement outside the back door, which had been kept ajar to allow some cool air to penetrate the stifling warmth of the room.

Fearing it was a fox, she hurried over to close it, but her attention was caught by the sound of voices, which sounded to her like a couple arguing. Liv strained to hear what was being said, then bit back a gasp as she realised that the fighting couple were none other than Jane and Mr Jackson.

"My dear Jane," Mr Jackson was speaking in a very calm, dispassionate voice. "I pray you will compose yourself, I have not asked you to commit murder. Merely to wait for me until I return from the South Americas."

"But that could be years."

Liv could hear the shake in her friend's voice, and she instinctively knew that Jane was holding back tears.

"Five years. Seven at the most," Liv could picture Mr Jackson waving away Jane's concerns with an impatient hand. Seven years was a long time to ask a woman to wait, Liv thought, especially when one was considered already on the shelf, as Jane was.

"I thought that this year," Jane sniffed loudly, her voice trembling, perilously verging on hysterics. "I thought this year that you would ask me to be your wife Alastair. I've spent so long waiting, and every time you let me down."

"You're acting in a most peculiar way, Jane," Mr Jackson sounded thoroughly annoyed, his every word ringing with impatience. "Honestly — I'm nearly reconsidering asking you to wait at all."

It took all of Liv's willpower, not to march out the back door and smack Mr Jackson resoundingly across his smug, pompous face. Luckily, Jane seemed to have had the same idea, for a ringing slap echoed across the night.

"I think you can deduce from that, Mr Jackson," Jane's voice sounded shocked, as though she could not believe what she had just done. "That I shan't be waiting for you. Though thank you for your most magnanimous offer."

Olive heard the sound of footsteps hurrying toward the side gate, and she quickly stepped away from the door. Jane, must have gone home, but Mr Jackson was still in the garden, and quite possibly could come in at any moment. Liv quickly returned to her tea tray, and when the entomologist slipped through the door, with a brief hello, she gave him a curt nod. He had been planning to leave at the end of the week, but Liv wondered if he would push his date of departure forward, after all the unpleasantness with Jane. She hoped so, for she would far prefer to have her friend about, than the dull Mr Jackson.

"I have tea," she called gaily, as she entered the drawing room. "Coffee for Mrs Actrol and hot milk for Beatrice."

Liv served the two older women first, while the twins poured for themselves and the Misses Devoy and Dunham. The four younger women were in high spirits, and much of the tea ended up on the carpet.

"I haven't had this much fun in years," Mrs Actrol said, wiping away tears as Liv handed her a steaming hot cup of black, bitter coffee. "Did you know, that a whole new set of bawdy songs have been created since I was a girl? Oh the things that people can make rhyme with Duke."

Liv smiled, through somewhat gritted teeth. She knew the limerick that Mrs Actrol was referring to —it was about her estranged husband. She had found it amusing when she had first heard it in London, but now that she knew something of Ruan and his late wife, she could not bear to hear it again.

"Do you know any different limericks Poppy?" she asked quickly, lest Mrs Actrol request she repeat it for Liv's pleasure. The young, blonde woman furrowed her brow, as she tried to think of another amusing poem.

"Oh I know one," Alexandra interjected, her eyes dancing with mischief. She stood, took her place at the centre of the room and took a deep breath, before beginning; "There once was a Viscount from Harrow, whose posterior was less than nar—oh!"

Alexandra broke off mid-word, to stare with alarm at the person who had just entered the drawing room. Fearing that it was the twins' Aunt Augusta, Liv whirled around.

"Gemini!" she heard Poppy whisper with excitement, behind her, but in truth the whole room seemed to have receded from Liv's vision, and all that she could see was the Duke of Everleigh. He, in turn, did not seem to see anyone else bar Liv; and he was looking at her in a way that expressed a mix of great displeasure and triumph, all at once.

"Your Grace," she heard herself say, averting her eyes from his penetrating gaze.

The women, who had previously been so cheerful, remained silent, as they watched the exchange between their hostess and the handsome intruder.

"Is anyone going to tell me what's going on?" Mrs Actrol finally said, impatience getting the better of her. "At my advanced age, I can't be expected to wait very long for explanations, I might not live long enough to hear them."

This, of course, was ridiculous, for Mrs Actrol was in perfect health, though Liv was grateful that she had spoken, for she herself had lost that ability the second her husband walked in the door.

"Mrs Actrol," Ruan bowed slightly in her direction, "I know your works, of course, but have never had the pleasure of meeting you. I'm afraid that our time together will be brief, however, for I am only here to fetch my wife and take her home."

"Your wife?"

Every lady in the room glanced at each other curiously; was the woman seated next to them the secret wife of the Duke of Everleigh? How exciting!

"Yes my wife," Ruan frowned in Olive's direction, his voice low and droll. "She seems to be labouring under the misapprehension that she is a boarding-house proprietress, and not a Duchess."

Liv didn't have to look up, to know that the faces of her guests were turned her way in shock. She heard a few gasps, and the word "Gemini" uttered several times, but kept her gaze locked on her husband's. He was not the only one who could stare menacingly, she thought grimly.

"If you would all be so kind," she said, struggling to keep her voice even,so as not to overly alarm her guests. "As to give the Duke and I some privacy. We have a few small matters that we need to discuss."

Ruan snorted at the word small, but stepped aside to allow the ladies of the house to file past him and out the door. Liv knew with certainty that they would all remain outside in the hallway, with their ears pressed against the door to see what they could hear. Once they had all left, she let out a sigh, and turned to face her husband.

"A few small matters?" Ruan cocked an eyebrow, his expression amused. Liv could see that he was in fact far from entertained by her choice of words, and that behind his exterior veneer of patience, he was seething with anger.

"A few small matters?" he repeated, his voice rising slightly as he approached her. It was like watching a predator ready to pounce on its prey, and Liv quickly took a step back behind an armchair so that it blocked his path.

"Our marriage is no small thing," he said, his eyes sweeping the armchair disdainfully, as if to let her know that it was a small obstacle that would not challenge his strength. "It is a legally binding contract, in which you swore, before God, that you would be mine until death do us part. And faking your own death does not count."

Liv bristled at his imperious tone; he still believed that he owned her, simply because he had won her hand in a game of cards.

"You forget, your Grace," she threw him a gaze that would have made most men quake in their boots, "That our marriage was not consummated, and that I am within my rights to seek an annulment."

"All I need is five minutes, and the matter of our unconsummated marriage will be remedied completely."

"Five minutes?" Liv arched an eyebrow, "That's hardly something to boast about, your Grace."

She watched as his blue eyes turned dark with anger, and for the first time since he had arrived she felt genuine fear. Why had she gone straight for the jugular? She should have known that a man like Ruan Ashford would not take having his lovemaking skills mocked.

"I have told you, my dear," he whispered, his eyes almost black. "That my name is Ruan, and I shall hear it from your lips before this night is out. And I can guarantee that when you say it, you will be screaming it in the throes of pleasure."

"You mean to force me?"

"In my life I have never forced a woman into my bed, and I'm not about to start with you."

With a simple kick of his polished Hessian, he upended the armchair between them, and before Liv could even think to react, he had closed the distance between them and taken her roughly into his arms.

"You are my wife." His voice was low and husky, and as he took her lips with his he emitted a growl that was filled with anger and need. If Liv had thought that their kisses on The Elizabeth had been passionate, this time they were even more so. He seemed to fill her every sense; the feel of his lips pressing insistently against hers, the taste of his kisses, his masculine scent filling her head and making her feel woozy with desire. He was right — there was no way that the Duke of Everleigh would ever have to force any woman into his bed, they would go willingly, begging even, for the chance to experience all the pleasure he promised.

"No!"

As his hands began to rove her body, Liv somehow found the reserves of strength she needed, despite her body's treacherous response to his touch, and she pushed hard against his chest, so that he staggered backward.

"I can't," she cried, her breath coming in short, shallow bursts, "I won't let you take this away from me."

"Take what?" Ruan's voice was laden with sarcasm. "A drafty boarding house in the back-end of nowhere?"

"No -my freedom," she replied, trying to steel herself against the ridicule she knew that he would pour on that statement. When he remained silent, she stole a look at him, and saw that his eyes were thoughtful.

"When you asked me why I married you, I said it was because I wanted a wife who challenged me," he said, with a hollow laugh. "Be careful what you wish for, isn't that what they say?"

"What about the lot that I landed? A husband I did not wish for at all," she retorted. She needed him to leave, soon, because despite her protests that he was not what she had wanted, now that he was here, she was filled with a need she had not known existed. Not until he kissed her.

"I'll show you to the door," she said, smoothing down the front of her dress, as much to calm her nerves as to straighten the material.

"I won't leave."

His voice was like thunder filling the room, and for a moment Liv felt genuine fear, until the door was pushed open and Polly came storming in. She held a pistol and her hand was steady as she pointed it directly at the Duke of Everleigh.

"I believe the Duchess asked you to leave, your Grace," Polly spoke mildly as if she was attending a tea-party, though she did not lower the weapon in her hand, despite the pleasantness of her demeanor. Liv stifled a cry of shock with her hands; she was sure that Ruan would lunge for her friend, but instead, the Duke gave an amused chuckle.

"Is this any way to greet your employer Miss Jenkins?"

Polly glanced sideways at Olive, her eyes full of apologies, before she replied; "You employed me to protect your wife, your Grace, and at the moment you are the biggest threat to her wellbeing. I do hope you understand."

"Oh, I understand completely," Ruan's blue eyes were resigned as he glanced at Olive, who stood rooted to the floor her mind reeling from the revelation that Ruan had sent Polly to spy on her. "I will take my leave tonight; but rest assured Olive, you will see me tomorrow."

With that he donned his hat, gave a small bow and swept angrily from the room, startling the ladies in the hallway, whose gasps could be heard from the drawing room. Olive ignored them and instead focused her attention on the woman standing opposite her, the woman who had purported to be her friend.

"You lied to me," she whispered, her eyes fixed on Polly's hand, which was gripping the pistol with a casual elegance that suggested more than a passing familiarity with holding fire arms.

"Aye," Polly gave a sigh, that seemed to encompass the weariness of the whole world. "I did, your Grace, and I apologise. But I can explain, if you'll let me."

"Why should I? You have betrayed me Polly; I don't think I can forgive you that."

"I'm not asking for forgiveness," Polly's voice was determined, and she sat down on the divan and gestured for Olive to sit in the chair opposite her. "I want to explain exactly what happened the night that Catherine Ashford died —and maybe then you can decide if you still wish to send the Duke away. For he is one of the most selfless men I have ever met, and I cannot leave until I plead his case with you."

Despite her reservations, Olive sat down, her curiosity to know more about the enigmatic Duke overpowering her anger.

"This had better be good," she said with a sniff, placing her hands primly on her lap as she waited for Polly to begin.

"It is," Polly held her gaze, "It's the true story of how your husband came to be known as the Duke of Ruin, and why that title is totally undeserved."

"You're back?"

Lord Deveraux was well and truly in his cups when Ruan stormed into the library of Jarvis House later that evening. He and Lord Payne were still sprawled on the chairs drinking brandy, and the only difference that Ruan could discern since leaving them a few hours ago, was that the decanter of alcohol was now nearly empty.

"Yes, it would seem I have to impose on your hospitality a bit longer, Deveraux. I hope you don't mind?"

Ruan could have returned to Pemberton Hall, which lay some thirty miles away, but he wanted to remain close to St. Jarvis —close to Olive. With a small nod of thanks, Ruan accepted a tumbler of brandy from Lord Deveraux, and sat down on a nearby chaise with a sigh.

"No luck then?" Lord Payne questioned, again displaying his utter lack of tact. If Ruan was the type of man who was easily offended, the young Lord's overly familiar tone would have grated on his nerves. As it was, it took a lot to offend Ruan, and there was a boyish charm about Lord Payne, that made one overlook his lazy manners.

"I was ordered out of the establishment at gun point," he replied shortly, earning a guffaw of amusement from Lord Payne.

"Lud," he put down his drink, and shook his blonde mop of hair in bemusement. "And I thought I had the worst luck with women, but you seem to be beating even me Everleigh. That's quite an accomplishment!"

"Glad to be of service."

If Payne had noted the dryness of Ruan's tone, he ignored it; instead he launched into a long tale of woe involving a mistress in Belgravia, a dressmaker's bill so extravagant it made even Ruan wince, and a black eye delivered in a fit of passion by a fiery actress, the traces of which still lingered on Payne's face.

"Having a mistress is supposed to be a resting activity," Julian snorted, as Payne's sad tale came to an end. "Not a pastime which leaves you battered and bruised."

"Unless that's the sort of thing you're into," Ruan quipped, then immediately wished he hadn't for Lord Payne launched into a long inquisition of what actions a man might ask a mistress to carry out if they were interested in that sort of thing.

Darkness had fallen by the tome Ruan finished his drink, and when his tumbler was empty he refused the next measure that Deveraux offered, instead standing up and stretching his weary body. His day had been long and it had not ended the way he had hoped it would —with Olive warming his bed. He frowned in annoyance; during the long ride from Southampton the thought of what he would do to Olive once he had her alone in his bedchamber had been foremost on his mind, and now he found himself filled with desire but with no outlet for it. He bid the two slightly sauced gentlemen goodnight, and went in search of a footman or another servant who might direct him to a bedchamber.

Jarvis House lay in darkness, but as Ruan made his way to the entrance hall, he saw a shaft of light emerging from a door that was slightly ajar. "Hello?" he knocked, pushing the door open.

He had expected to perhaps find the housekeeper or the butler ensconced inside the tiny sitting room, but instead it was Jane, curled up by the fire reading a rather large, dusty looking book.

"Your Grace," Jane looked up, startled as he entered the room. "I thought you were returning to Pemberton Hall?"

"A slight change of plans," he replied, and nodded at the book in her hands. "Interesting bed time reading?"

Jane wrinkled her nose, shook her head and placed the book aside. From his vantage point Ruan could read the title: Native Insects of the British Isles.

"I wouldn't have pegged you as an insect enthusiast," he commented, and to his surprise Jane frowned darkly.

"Oh, I'm not," she said firmly, "Can't stand the wretched things. Tell me your Grace, did my brother manage to stop drinking for long enough to find you a room for the night?"

She gave a loud sigh of annoyance when the Duke shook his head to her question.

"I pray you will forgive his bad manners," Jane said, rising from her chair and gesturing for Ruan to follow her. She took a candle, and led him through the dark, winding halls of Jarvis House. He followed her up the stairs, past rows of portraits of Deverauxs past, and down a long corridor to one of the guest suites.

"If I had known you were staying, I would have had one of the chamber maids light the fire," Jane said apologetically as she left him outside the door. "If you're cold, I could wake one of them to do it for you?"

Even though she had offered, her tone was reluctant, and Ruan knew that the soft-hearted Jane would have been loathe to wake a sleeping maid in the dead of night to light a fire —even for a Duke.

"I'm sure I'll be perfectly fine, thank you, Jane," he replied easily; in truth the night was very mild and Ruan knew that he wouldn't even need bedclothes. Though that wasn't the type of thing one said to a lady in a dark corridor. "Thank you again for allowing me to stay, I need to remain close to St. Jarvis for the foreseeable future."

"Is it true that Olive-" Jane hesitated, glancing at him nervously as though trying to ascertain what his reaction might be.

"Olive is my wife," Ruan confirmed, wondering how Deveraux had described the situation to his sister. No doubt he had embellished the tale, for Jane looked even more nervous now that he had confirmed the fact.

"I hope you don't mind my impertinence, your Grace," she continued, still looking nervous but determined to say her piece. "But if that is the case, then why are you here and not with her?"

"Olive has no desire for me to be anywhere near her," Ruan gave a hollow laugh which made Jane flinch. It must have sounded more bitter than he had intended it, and indeed he felt more bitter than he had thought was possible. Olive's rejection had truly rankled him, both his pride and his heart, which he had not realised was so involved in the whole situation until it had begun to ache with loneliness. "She has no desire to be my Duchess, and I wouldn't be too wrong in saying that she loathes me most thoroughly."

"Oh, dear."

Jane's summation of the situation was so mild and polite that Ruan almost laughed. Oh, dear indeed.

"Do you think perhaps she suffered some sort of shock after what happened on The Elizabeth?" Jane wondered aloud.

"I think she was more shocked by the events that happened before we even boarded the ruddy ship," Ruan conceded; he was starting to realise that his behaviour in gaining Olive's hand might have been slightly overbearing. Jane gave him an inquisitive look, and reluctantly Ruan shared the story of how he had come to win Olive in a game of chance, after having carefully orchestrated the situation so that Lord Greene would have no choice but to wager his daughter's hand.

"If she actually liked you, the whole thing would be rather romantic," Jane quipped, once Ruan had finished his sorry tale. "Love at first sight, winning her hand —it's almost like something from a novel!"

"Yes, but as we have deduced Jane, my wife doesn't like me. Not even a little bit."

"Well, you could start by trying to make yourself more likable," she suggested brightly, "Honestly your Grace, I've never known a man try so hard to be so unpopular —when underneath your prickly exterior, you're ever so nice."

Ever so nice was not a phrase that was often used to describe the Duke of Everleigh, and while Ruan knew that he was often high-handed and imperious, he felt it was behaviour befitting of a man of his station.

"I am a Duke," he retorted, a little sullenly, "I can't spend my days mollycoddling people so that they don't feel intimidated by me."

"No," Jane seemed to be suppressing a smile as she watched his reaction to her suggestion, "But perhaps you could try not intimidating your wife? That might be a better tactic when dealing with matters of the heart. Good night, your Grace."

Ruan watched her slip down the dark corridor his gaze thoughtful. Jane Deveraux was an intelligent woman, and there was no denying that his current strategy of overwhelm and command was not winning him any affection from his estranged wife. Could a campaign of courtship win out instead? He frowned; roses and sweet words were not exactly his style, but as he opened the door to his bedroom, and spotted the empty bed, he reasoned he would try anything to win Olive over.

"I was twenty years old when the Duke hired me to care for his wife," Polly began slowly, her brow furrowed as she recalled the story that had begun many years ago. "I first met his Grace in Bristol, where he kindly employed me in the offices of his shipping company —I was in charge of paying the wages and the like to the sailors. A rough lot some of them were."

"I didn't think this was a retelling of your life story Polly," Olive snapped, trying to quell the guilt she felt at her rude behaviour. She tried to remind herself that Polly had lied to her, and had been paid to spy on her by her husband, and for a moment her rudeness felt justified.

"No need for that, your Grace," Polly replied mildly, unperturbed by Olive's uncharacteristically bad-tempered behaviour. "I was merely trying to illustrate why his Grace chose me as his wife's companion — it was on account of the fact that I had experience dealing with hot-headed males on a day to day basis. The late Duchess had gone through a dozen companions before I came along."

Olive remained silent as she considered this; surely Catherine Ashford hadn't been so greatly disturbed that the Duke couldn't have found a proper lady to cope with her behaviour?

"When I arrived at Pemberton Hall," Polly continued, ignoring Olive's foot which was tapping with impatience, "Her Grace was in a bad way. Her Lady's maids had all left, due to all the violent outbursts, and I dare say she hadn't bathed in weeks. She was hard to deal with, screaming and raging one minute then as meek as a baby the next, but I persevered. I was used to difficult behaviour, what with looking after Emily all my life."

"Emily?"

Olive hadn't wanted to ask any questions, or protract their conversation any longer than was necessary, but her interest was piqued.

"My sister," Polly eyed her defiantly, "She is not, as some might say, the full shilling. Though that's all that some would get to say, if they spoke ill of her around me."

Polly wore an expression that Liv thought might be similar to the one a tigress might display if anybody threatened her cubs. The fierce love and protectiveness that Polly felt for her sister was evident, and Olive felt a stab of envy; she had always wanted a sister, and she wondered what it would be like to have someone as strong as Polly always there to protect her.

"Where was I?" Polly ran a distracted hand through her hair, as though to push away the feelings for her sister while she concentrated on her tale. "Oh yes; the late Duchess was in quite a state when I first arrived, but after a few weeks of tough-love, she was much better —and remained that way for quite some time, until Charles Birmingham returned."

Charles Birmingham, Liv knew, was the man that the Duke of Everleigh had killed in a duel, the man who had been his late wife's lover.

"Oh, he was a bad 'un," Polly scowled darkly, as she recalled the deceased man. "And her Grace, the moment she saw him, seemed to forget all the bad things that he had done to her before, and fell under his spell like that."

Polly clicked her fingers, to indicated just how quickly the late Duchess had been bewitched by Birmingham, but Liv ignored her, for something else had caught her attention.

"What do you mean, all the things he had done before?" she asked slowly.

Polly flushed, evidently that was part of the tale that she hadn't intended to mention. Seeing Liv's look of determination, however, she heaved a great sigh.

"I don't wish to speak ill of my late mistress," she whispered, glancing at the door to make sure that it was shut. "But Birmingham had seduced her and abandoned her, years ago, leaving her in a very difficult situation. It was why the Duke married her in the first place — to save her reputation."

Liv gasped; she had not known this, and she couldn't imagine why a man of Everleigh's title and status would feel obliged to marry a woman pregnant with a child that was not his.

"He loved her," as though reading her thoughts, Polly spoke again. "Not love like romantic love in the poems, but in the way that I love Emily. They had been friends for all their childhood, and when she wrote to him to explain what had happened he arrived in St. Jarvis a few days after he'd received the letter, and they were married the next day. He simply wanted to protect her."

Protect her by giving her his name, Olive thought, shocked by the selflessness her husband had displayed. He had not cared for lineage or social gossip, he had simply wanted to save his friend from ridicule and scorn. This image of Ruan as a man who would give up everything to protect the people he loved was hard to marry with the obnoxious Duke she had wed, just a few short weeks ago.

"And the baby?"

"Born an angel," Polly whispered, "The Duke said that after she lost the little girl, Catherine spiraled into a complete depression, that only ended when I arrived. Can you imagine how hard it must have been for him, for I didn't land on the doorstep of Pemberton Hall until two years later."

Liv shook her head; she could not picture what Everleigh had done for those years, caring for a woman who was mad with grief. Other families, she knew, sent relatives to asylums —swept them under the carpet like they did not exist— but Ruan had kept Catherine safely at home.

"Where was I?" Polly shook her head, attempting to focus for they had both deviated from the original plot of the tale. "Oh, yes. Mr Birmingham arrived back in St Jarvis, and almost overnight, her Grace was back to suffering violent mood swings. I did not know what was wrong with her for many months, and the Duke was away at sea. Then things began to disappear, her Grace's jewels, some of the silverware; small things at first, then gradually even the other servants began to comment on it, and I knew that I was not imagining things."

"Was it Birmingham?"

"Of course, who else? But for a while I think people suspected it was I, until Mrs Hogg, the housekeeper saw him sneaking in one evening."

"What happened then?" Liv asked curiously.

"Oh, all hell broke loose," Polly frowned, "I could not forbid her from seeing him, it wasn't my place, I was just a paid companion and she was a Duchess. Now that he had been spotted, he would call whenever he felt like it. For weeks and weeks he plagued her, writing love letters one day then initiating blazing rows the next. He held the threat of leaving again above her head like a guillotine. The poor woman was shaking from the moment she woke, to when she fell asleep. Then his Grace returned, and I informed him of what was happening..."

Polly trailed off, looking rather uncomfortable at the memory.

"And what happened then?" Liv prompted softly.

"Oh her Grace soon found out who had snitched on her," Polly was pale, her eyes focused on the wall and not Olive as she recalled what had happened. "She lunged at me, and began to choke me. I could not push her off, her fury was so great. If the Duke had not heard my screams, I would be dead. He pulled her off me, but even he struggled with her, and he's a big man, as you well know. Her Grace was sobbing, hysterical — and then she confessed that she had given Birmingham a vast sum of money, for him to purchase a home for the pair of them, but he had disappeared again. Imagine, the poor thing believed the lying swine, even after all he'd done to her."

Olive saw genuine pity for her mistress in Polly's eyes, despite the woman having nearly killed her. The rest of the story Liv half knew already; the Duke had found Birmingham in a tavern in Bristol, and challenged him to a duel. The ton had all thought it was because Everleigh was jealous of the man, but it had all been revenge for what he had done to his wife.

"News reached Pemberton Hall, that the Duke had shot Birmingham dead," Polly continued, "And I cannot say that I was sorry. I tried to keep it from her Grace, but somehow she found out. It must have been from a stable boy, or one of the lower maids, for they were nervous of her position and didn't understand that she was to be lied to if necessary."

"And how did her Grace take the news?" Olive asked, already knowing the answer to her question.

"Not well, not well at all."

Polly stood up, and began pacing the length of the drawing room. She was visibly agitated and as she glanced at Liv, her eyes were misty with tears.

"I must ask you to promise that you will take this next piece of information to your grave," Polly said solemnly, and wide-eyed Olive nodded her agreement.

"Her Grace did not take the news well, as you can imagine. She wept and raged the whole day long, finally she fell asleep, but I was so worried for her that I slept in her bedchamber on a chair. I must have dozed off, for the next thing I knew I was woken by the sound of the door slamming shut. I raced after her, but I was too late. I rushed out into the hallway, and she was climbing over the banisters on the landing, but I was too far away to pull her back. I saw her jump, Olive, it was an awful sight to witness."

Olive paled; she could well imagine the horror that had filled poor Polly as she watched her mistress jump to her death.

"She landed on the marble tiles of the entrance hall," Polly winced, as though remembering the sound. "I knew that she was dead the moment that I reached her. Mrs Hogg, who had been closing up the house for the night, witnessed the whole thing too. We were in an awful state, we didn't know what to do and then the Duke arrived home, just moments after she had leapt."

"But he said he was there?" Olive interrupted, her brow furrowed with thought. "I read it in the papers, he said that he saw his wife trip and fall down the stairs."

"No one would question the word of a Duke," Polly shrugged, "That was what he told us. He wanted to give Catherine a proper burial in a graveyard; he wanted to protect her from cruel gossip even in death."

Olive was silent as she absorbed this. Ruan had not been present when his wife had died, and yet had claimed to be so in order to preserve her honour; the Church would not bury a suicide on Holy ground. He must have known that after the incident with Birmingham that people might suspect him of having a hand in Catherine's death, and yet he had gone ahead with his plan. The Duke of Ruin had ruined his own reputation, to preserve Catherine Ashford's. The irony was not lost on Olive, who gave Polly a wan smile.

"I can see that I was wrong about his Grace," she said, and the other woman's shoulders visibly sagged with relief. "I shall not tell a soul what you have told me Polly, I swear it."

"Not even the Duke?"

"Would he not want me to know?"

Polly snorted with amusement; "His Grace is a good man, but even I'd be the first to admit that he's pig-headed and stubborn about letting people know he's got a soft side."

"Even his wife?" Olive wondered aloud.

"Is that what you are?"

Olive let the loaded question linger in the air unanswered. After what she had heard, she knew that the Duke of Everleigh was not a bad man —but did that mean that she wanted to be his Duchess

Ruan frowned as he waited for someone to answer the door he had just knocked on. He felt like a fool standing on the front step of the boarding house, with a bouquet of posies hidden behind his back. He was gripping them so hard that he was certain the stems would have turned to mush by the time he handed them over to Olive.

The door creaked open and Polly's familiar face peered out, wreathing into a smile as she saw that it was he.

"Good morning, your Grace," she sang brightly, ushering him inside. "'Tis another beautiful sunny day, is it not?"

"It is," Ruan tried not to sound too impatient; he was not there to discuss the weather. He followed Polly into the drawing room that he had stormed into blind with rage the night before. Today, in the late morning sunshine, he saw that the room was elegantly appointed with fine furnishings and dozens of framed paintings lining the walls. Polly gestured for him to sit and turned to leave to fetch Olive, but stopped when the Duke addressed her.

"I take it the Duchess holds no ill will against you for your deception?"

"Only a small bit, your Grace," Polly bit her lip nervously, "And I hope that you hold no ill will against me for the way that I asked you to leave?"

"You're not the first person to point a loaded pistol at me," Ruan replied with a short laugh, "And I dare say you won't be the last —but Polly?"

Polly glanced at him nervously.

"Don't do it again."

Ruan hid a smile as the young woman bobbed her head and positively fled the room. He truly was not annoyed with Polly, he had known that she would not actually shoot him, and she had merely been doing the job he had instructed her to do — protect his wife. Ruan stood and began to pace the drawing room as he waited for Olive to arrive. He felt like a complete and utter dolt; his heart was racing, his palms were sweaty and he was as jumpy as young blood about to attend his first ball. Honestly, he shook his head in annoyance, it was ridiculous to feel this nervous — he was a Duke for goodness sake!

The self-affirmation fled his head however, when Olive slipped into the room and gave a discreet cough to let him know she was there. Ruan whirled around, and instantly his mouth went dry. She was dressed in a simple day dress, with her red curls piled atop her head, and the vision she created was mesmerising. His eyes strayed to her plump lips, which were slightly open as though she wanted to speak but could not find the words.

"I brought you these."

He crossed the room in two long strides and thrust the rather sorry looking bunch of posies toward his wife.

"I'm sorry they're not more grand," he continued, feeling slightly abashed as he glanced at the flowers, which were now visibly wilting in Olive's hand. "But Deveraux does not have a hot-house, and his gardener was reluctant to allow me to take anything else from the flower beds."

"You picked them yourself?"

Ruan flushed slightly as Olive perfectly arched an eyebrow in question, she had succeeded in making him feel two inches tall with just one movement. "Well yes, I was rather going for the 'it's the thought that counts' approach to flower giving, and ordering one of the servants to fetch them for me seemed to be missing the mark somewhat."

"They're lovely, thank you," she finally replied, walking over to the sideboard and carefully arranging the posies into a vase. "And thank you for the thought, it was most kind."

She turned then to look at him, and she appeared to him like an angel, bathed in soft morning light. Her green eyes were inquisitive, and she unconsciously bit her lips nervously, rendering Ruan speechless with desire as he observed her. Oh what he wouldn't give to bite down on that lip.

"Why are you here?" she finally asked, turning to the sideboard to fiddle with a small ornament.

"I had rather hoped that we could start again, from the beginning." Ruan cleared his throat, wishing he could make his request sound more like he was asking, and less like he was demanding. Ducal habits were hard to shed, and he knew that he sounded a tad commanding, but he continued on none the less. "It is customary for a gentleman to call on a lady he desires the morning after they have met at a ball. I was hoping, that perhaps, you might deign to pretend that it is the morning after we first met at Lady Jersey's, and allow me to court you properly, as I should have done from the off."

"How intriguing," Ruan tried not to scowl as Olive's eyes danced with amusement while she spoke. "There is only one problem your Grace, I'm not sure that after your abominable behaviour at Lady Jersey's if I would have been at home to you, had you decided to call..."

"So you are suggesting that we must go even further back, and pretend we have never met at all?"

Ruan had the definite feeling that Olive was making fun of him. She seemed to be fighting back a smile and turned her gaze away from his, as she pondered his suggestion.

"Oh yes," she said very seriously, so seriously that Ruan knew she was definitely making fun of him. "They say one only gets a single chance to make a first impression, and I rather fear that the one you made that night was most alarming. Perhaps if we could orchestrate a faux formal introduction, we could start again. Though how we could manage that when there is no one here to introduce us is beyond me..."

"Are you mocking me?"

To Ruan's surprise Olive gave a giddy laugh, and nodded her head. She covered her mouth, to hide her wide smile, as she glanced at him almost affectionately.

"Oh, I am, your Grace," she laughed, "And I pray you forgive me, but your face is a picture. I dare say not many people ever tease you."

"They don't," Ruan grumbled, but inwardly he felt a jolt of pleasure. It was true, few people had ever teased him, bar the ribald comments that men often made to each other, yet Olive's light tone and dancing eyes made him wonder what he had been missing out on all this time.

"Would you like me to stop?"

His wife arched an eyebrow again, and she seemed to be holding her breath, as though his answer might make or break her.

"No," he shook his head slowly and held her gaze, "Though I'd rather you take your unique brand of humour outside with me for a ride. I have a Tilbury outside that I borrowed from Deveraux, as well as a picnic basket filled with cold meats and the like."

"A Tilbury?"

She was teasing him again, and this time Ruan felt genuine embarrassment. He had not driven a Gig since he was a young lad, but Deveraux and Payne had taken the much more fashionable Phaeton off to Truro for a spin.

"It's not my usual mode of transport," he muttered, "Though it will get us safely to the cliffs, which are a magnificent spot for taking lunch."

"As long as you promise not to push me off them," Olive said, apparently in agreement with his plan, for she made for the door. She paused as she reached the door, her face awash with horror at her faux pas; "Not that I think you would, of course. That wasn't what I meant."

"I didn't kill Catherine," he replied simply, and much to his surprise she gave him a compassionate look and whispered; "I know."

His heart skipped a beat at her words.

The Duke of Everleigh was quiet for most of their short journey along the cliff road, only breaking his silence to point out places of interest. The ruined watch-tower from centuries ago, an area along the cliffs where there had been a large rock-slide a few years before, the place where Ruan had learnt how to gallop a horse for the first time. This last image gave Olive cause to smile; she could not imagine the large, intimidating man beside her as a small boy. His masculinity was so overwhelming that it was hard to picture him embodying any other form than the imposing, muscular one he now possessed. Which of course was ridiculous, Olive scolded herself, he had not entered the world at six foot four.

"What was it like?" she asked, as the Gig rounded a corner and a breathtaking view of the sea was revealed, stretching for miles, as far as the eye could see. "Growing up here? It must have been idyllic."

"It was," Ruan nodded, "In many ways it was perfect. My father sent me here most summers, and winter was spent at the Ducal seat in Avon. Everleigh Hall is much larger than Pemberton and far less homely, so I preferred Cornwall and the freedom it offered me."

"Did he send you alone?" Olive tried to keep the distaste from her voice; her own childhood memories of summer were filled with family— her mother, her cousins, even her wretched father who had not been so bad in those days.

"Yes," Ruan looked at her with surprise, having caught the censure of her tone. "After my mother left, my father could barely stand to look at me. He had his heir, he cared little for raising me and left that to my governess."

"That's awful."

Ruan caught her tone of pity and gave her an amused smile.

"My father was not a very nice man," he shrugged, "So leaving me with the governess was a mutually beneficial arrangement. She was a wonderful woman, I lacked for nothing. And I had great friends here, in St. Jarvis, to keep me company."

"Oh, yes," Liv smiled, "I have heard that you, Somerset and Deveraux were considered the three musketeers of the area."

The Duke snorted; "I doubt we ever did anything as remarkable or heroic as The Musketeers, bar frighten a fisherman or two, but the three of us were inseparable —and Catherine, of course."

"Was Catherine your Constance?" Liv ventured, thinking that like the heroine from Dumas's novel both had met tragic ends.

"Actually," Ruan's voice was low and filled with nostalgia, "Catherine was always closer with Lavelle than I. Deveraux and I had wagers placed on when they would wed, but once Somerset came of age and left for London, he forgot about her almost completely. Which sounds hard-hearted, but London offers a veritable buffet of delights for a young, well-heeled man, and in one's first few years in town it is easy to be led astray."

"You weren't led astray though," Olive countered, thinking of what Polly had told her. Ruan too had gone to London, but had returned when Catherine had summoned him to rescue her.

"It might surprise you," Ruan said with a laugh, as he pulled the horse in at a bend in the road. "But I tend to be sentimental when it comes to the people I love. I find it hard to forget them, even when I try."

Was he speaking of Catherine? Olive watched him closely as he disembarked the Gig and held his hand out to help her down. There was an ease to his movements, a lightness to his step, and yet his eyes were sad and thoughtful.

"This is one of my favourite places in the whole world," he said conversationally, as he untied the horse from the gig and tethered her to a nearby fence post. "We'll follow the path down the cliffs, to where the castle ruins are. There's a small cove which is utterly beautiful, you'll see it when we get there."

He lifted a basket, which appeared weighed down with foodstuff, out of the gig and gestured for her to follow him. Olive scrambled after her husband, along the stony path, which ran down the side of the cliffs. The climb was steep, but not arduous, and when they reached the castle ruins, Olive could see why Ruan loved the place so. The old, crumbling walls of the castle were built along the jagged rocks of the headland. Some walls were still half standing, and as they passed by Olive caught glimpses of the sea through the Baluster windows that still remained. She followed Ruan across what must have once been a courtyard, and down stone steps which had been built into the cliff wall centuries before.

Beneath them there was a small cove, with a white, sandy beach, and turquoise water lapping against the shore.

"Oh," she gasped, as she took in the beauty, "This must be what Italy is like!"

"Italy has nothing on Castle Cove," Ruan said dismissively. He took her hand as she negated the last of the stone steps, which were slippery with seaweed, and Olive felt a shiver of desire as his skin made contact with hers. When he dropped her hand to set the basket down on the soft, white sand, she felt almost bereft. How had her feelings toward him changed so drastically overnight? True, she had desired him even when she detested him, but now that she knew more about his past, her longing for him felt less conflicted and she did not try to fight it.

"Jane kindly arranged all this," Ruan said cheerfully as he unpacked a blanket and spread it out for them to sit on. Liv sank down and folded her hands primly on her lap as she watched the Duke unpack plates and pile them high with strawberries, cheeses and cold-meats. He had removed his jacket and rolled up his shirtsleeves so that his tanned, muscular forearms were on display. As he handed Liv her plate, she noted that his hands, while large, were elegant and that he wore the ring that she had stolen from him on his index finger.

"Your friend in the pawnshop sang like a canary," he said wryly, as he caught where her gaze was focused. There was no animosity in his voice for her having sold what was probably a precious family heirloom, but still she felt guilt at what she had done.

"I'm so sorry," she said, setting down her plate on the blanket, "I should not have taken it —and of course I will pay the money back to you—"

"Don't even try, or I will be very annoyed," Ruan interrupted, his eyes narrowed. "You owe me nothing, Olive."

The way that he spoke her name, so tenderly, filled Olive with warmth. She dropped her eyes to her lap and began fidgeting with her hands, as she tried to summon up the courage to ask him the question she had wanted to ask since the moment her father told her she was engaged to him.

"Why did you set about winning me in a card game?" she finally asked, raising her head so that she could look at his face. "Why did you not simply call on me and state your intentions?"

"I was afraid that you would say no."

The Duke delivered this statement in a very matter of fact way, but Olive could see that the tips of his ears had reddened with embarrassment.

"And then I had one of my business contacts find out what he could about your father, and it became clear that your situation was perilous," he continued, giving a shrug, "I could not simply leave you with him, and I was afraid that someone else might have the same idea as me, and use you as—as—"

"Leverage to pay his debts," Olive finished his sentence and gave a small snort of derision. "Thank you for the compliment your Grace, but I was never considered that much of a catch that any man would take me over the money my father owed. Money won out, every time."

"Then those men were fools," Ruan was vehement, "To not see what I saw."

Olive did not ask him what it was that he saw in her, for she could tell by his eyes which were hazy with lust and desire, just what it was that he wanted. Her own heart was pounding erratically in her chest, and a loaded silence fell between them, during which the only sound to be heard was the gentle lapping of the waves on the shore. He thought he was protecting me by stealing me away from my Father; Liv felt lightheaded at the realisation. No one, since her mother's death, had cared that much for her well-being. Though the way that he had gone about acquiring her hand still rankled.

"I wish that you had just asked me," she said morosely, popping a strawberry into her mouth to prevent herself from nibbling on her lip with anxiety.

"Is it too late to ask you now?"

His eyes held hers as she considered her response. One picnic did not make a great romance, she reasoned, but his idea to start over, from the beginning, showed that they might find a way. He was a good man, she knew this now, and he was so handsome it was sinful...but did she love him?

"It is too early yet, your Grace," she eventually replied, affecting a flippant air. "For you only called on me just this very morning, and a woman cannot accept a proposal of marriage from a man she has not even danced with."

Ruan's eyes narrowed speculatively and a flash of emotion crossed his face. "Then I must find a ball, my dear, and whisk you off your feet post-haste."

"A ball in St. Jarvis?" Liv raised a disbelieving eyebrow. "It cannot be done, your Grace."

"Anything is possible," Ruan replied, taking her hand and lifting it to his lips. "When it's done in pursuit of a beautiful woman."

"A ball! What a spiffing idea, old chap."

Lord Payne was the only person who met Ruan's suggestion that the Deverauxs hold a ball, with any modicum of enthusiasm. Jane looked positively pained at the idea and her brother more than a little bewildered.

"But," Lord Deveraux frowned, "You hate balls. You hate society. You hate being polite to society. I just don't understand your reasons, Everleigh."

"If I am to return to Pemberton hall," Ruan said slowly, searching for a reason that wasn't as embarrassing as telling Deveraux he simply wished to dance with his wife. "I would like to be publicly welcomed by society. I know it's a lot to ask of you, when you have already done so much…"

He trailed off and adopted what he hoped was a piteous look, rather than the irritation he felt. He was used to people agreeing with his ideas straight away, not questioning them. Jane was right, he thought, he was far too used to being an over-entitled Duke.

"What a good idea," Payne's boyish face lit up, as he swallowed Ruan's dreadful reasoning. "After all that ghastly business with the late Duchess it would be a good idea to test the waters before you returned permanently. I say, maybe there'll be a few eligible young ladies for me to peruse —I received another letter from my mother today, warning me that Father is making rumblings about marrying me off."

"I'm afraid my Lord, that I am the only single lady for miles, so I pray you lower your expectations for the night."

Lord Payne glanced at Jane in surprise, her droll tone having elicited a smile from Ruan.

"Well if you are the bar against which all the single ladies of Cornwall are to be compared, then it is set very high indeed, Lady Jane," the young, blonde man said gallantly. Jane flushed, and Ruan thought that she looked rather pleased, until her brother gave a disparaging snort at the notion. Honestly, when had Deveraux become such a boor?

"Then it's settled," Jane valiantly ignored her brother's bad manners, and turned to Ruan with a smile, "Now that Lord Payne knows not to expect a crush of beautiful debutants, we are in agreement. I shall notify the housekeeper to have the ballroom aired out, and I'll set about sending out the invitations."

"Jolly good," Payne smiled at the bespectacled young woman, "I shall help you write them,to save your hand from aching."

"Cornwall society is rather small, my Lord, it shan't take more than an hour. Though thank you for your offer."

Ruan got the impression that Jane was less than entranced by the idea of spending any time alone with Lord Payne, though the young buck seemed to miss the message in her words. "No I'd like to help Jane, and if it won't take long then you could, perhaps, help me to pen a letter to my mother. I need someone who has a good way with words, and I've rather a lot of explaining to do, what with the carriage accident and everything else…"

His voice faded, as the two exited the room, leaving Ruan and Deveraux alone in the library.

"Shall we invite Lord Keyford?" Deveraux's tone was deliberately light, for he knew that it was a heavy question. Ruan thought for a moment, before answering. What Lavelle had told him in Southampton had convinced him that Keyford was the man behind the numerous attacks on his person, and perhaps a staid country ball would be the best place to observe his late wife's father?

"Ask him in person," Ruan suggested, relieved when Deveraux nodded in agreement with his idea. "Let him know that I'll be here. If he comes, he comes. If not…"

If not, then perhaps Lord Keyford was the man behind the attacks. Ruan excused himself to take a walk, fetching his coat and hat from his bedchamber, before venturing out into the soft evening air. Jarvis House was a mere five minutes from the village, and Ruan gently strolled along the path, appreciating the peace of the evening, and the sounds of birds and insects in the hedgerow. The church of the parish of St. Jarvis was perched at the top of the hill, which ran down to the village. Like many other buildings in the locale, it was built from Cornish granite, and was surrounded by a slate wall. The churchyard was tidy, with an abundance of speedwells and figworts swaying in the light breeze. Ruan opened the gate, and followed the stone path around to the back of the church, where the graveyard was. Many new headstones had appeared since he had last visited, and he paused to read the names of those who had died in recent years. He felt his chest tighten as he approached Catherine's grave; at the head there was a simple granite headstone, which was inscribed with her name and the date of her death. He hunkered down before the stone, and as he did so he saw two roses had been laid there, quite recently, by the looks of how fresh they were. Ruan lifted one, and examined it curiously. It was a fine, long-stemmed rose, he knew by the quality of it that it must have been grown in a hot-house. It certainly hadn't come from Jarvis House, he thought, remembering his pathetic bunch of posies. Would Lord Keyford have left it? Ruan thought on what he knew of his father in law; Keyford had been a mean, tight individual, who had shown very little love to his only legitimate child during her lifetime. Perhaps, though, her death had filled him with remorse?

Ruan sighed; he would probably never know who had left the roses—though he could rule out most of the villagers, who would not have the type of money for such sentimental frivolities. He rested his hand on the headstone, and lowered his head to say a short prayer for his late wife. He had not known, when he was two and twenty, what he was taking on when he married Catherine. It had been akin to adopting a child; she was so vulnerable and helpless. He had tried to protect her, both from outside influences and the horrors that inflicted her internally, but he had failed. After her death he had been filled with sorrow, grief and guilt —and the guilt was made worse by the fact that, once some time had passed, he felt a sense of relief. This, more than anything, had convinced him that the rumours about him were true: he was a monster. The only person he had confided this to was Polly, and he had expected to receive a thorough dressing down from the straight talking Northerner. Instead he had found comfort, for she had merely told him that caring for someone —as she did for Emily and he had for Catherine—was not a straightforward business.

"Everything you did, you did because you loved Catherine, and wanted to protect her," she had soothed him. "And you did right by her, at great personal sacrifice to your own needs and wishes. Love is not an easy emotion your Grace; it's a million feelings all rolled into one, good and bad. Caring for Catherine was difficult, there's no harm in admitting that it was not all a bed of roses, for you do yourself a great disservice by pretending that it was."

His knees creaked slightly as he rose, and he began the short journey back to Jarvis House. As he exited the churchyard, he stole a glance down the path that led to the village. He could see the boarding house from here, and the lights blazed merrily in the windows. In Olive, he felt that he might find some redemption, if only she would let him be the husband that he knew he could be.

Perhaps this was a bad idea, Ruan thought, his stomach clenching as he guided the horses up the drive of Pemberton Hall. Olive sat, ram-rod straight, beside him, and Polly sat silently beside her. He had innocuously suggested, the day before, that his wife might like to visit his childhood home, and Olive had jumped at the idea. When he had collected her at the boarding house that morning, he discovered why: Polly wanted to see her sister.

Ruan had felt like a selfish git as he helped the Northern lass into the gig. He had been so preoccupied with Olive, that he had forgotten how much Polly probably missed young Emily, whom she was rarely separated from. Though she had probably found consolation in the fact that Emily been left in the care of the very able Mrs Hogg, who doted on the young girl.

The Housekeeper and Emily's sister stood at the door to greet them as Ruan steered the gig to the front steps of the house. He waved hello, before hopping out and assisting Olive and Polly from the vehicle.

"Polly!"

Young Emily, who now that Ruan thought on it was probably nearly twenty, tore down the front steps and launched herself at her elder sister. Polly staggered backwards at the force with which Emily threw herself on her, but she did not fall, merely wrapped her arms around her sister in a warm hug.

"Oh, I have missed you," Emily said, as she drew away from the embrace, "I have a new pet chicken, called Maisie. Mrs Hogg says her eggs are magical, though I told her not to be silly, eggs aren't magical only fairies are."

"Indeed her eggs are," the stout housekeeper called, as the group ascended the front steps of the house. "They make the finest puddings known to man, and I have one cooling in the kitchen for after luncheon, your Grace."

"Thank you Mrs Hogg," Ruan replied, casting a warm smile at the woman whose food had been the highlight of his childhood, "Allow me to introduce—"

He paused abruptly; what on earth was he supposed to introduce Olive as? The woman he had married, but had failed to bed? His poor housekeeper would drop dead if he shared that bit of information with her!

"Olive," his wife smiled at the housekeeper, neatly side-stepping Ruan's discomfort. "It's wonderful to meet you Mrs Hogg, I have heard so much about you and Pemberton Hall. Many people in St Jarvis have told me it's the most beautiful house to be found in all of Cornwall."

Mrs Hogg preened with pleasure at this statement, and led Olive inside, pointing out the different architectural merits of Pemberton Hall as they went. Polly and Emily discreetly said their goodbyes to the Duke, and disappeared across the manicured lawns to their small cottage. Ruan watched the pair for a moment, obviously giddy and in high spirits, his heart aching. What would it be like to know love as unconditional as the two Jenkins sisters shared? He had never known, even as a child, what it was like to have someone love him so. His memories of his mother were hazy at best, and while he had a few images of her kissing and hugging him, he wasn't entirely sure that he hadn't made them up. His father had always held him at arm's length, and as a boy he had longed for affection that wasn't provided by a dutiful staff member.

If I have children, he vowed as he watched Polly and Emily disappear from sight, I shall let them know that they are loved. He felt a stab of protectiveness for his yet fictitious offspring, and hastily followed his wife and housekeeper inside. There would be no children if he couldn't persuade Olive to return to the marriage bed.

His wife and Mrs Hogg were still in the entrance hall, viewing the many portraits that lined the wall.

"This is the late Duke," Mrs Hogg said, waving a hand at an intimidating, gilt framed portrait of Ruan's father. There was little resemblance between father and son, the Fifth Duke of Everleigh had been fair, while his son had favoured his mother's dark colouring. "And this is His Grace, ooh he must be only four or five in this, with the late Duchess. Wasn't she beautiful?"

Ruan remained silent as he watched Olive take a step closer to the painting of him and his mother. Her face seemed to soften as she viewed the image of him as a child; Ruan felt a momentary pang of embarrassment, for in the painting he was dressed in foppish pantaloons and his hair was long and curly, like a girls.

"You were adorable, your Grace," she said finally, glancing at him with warmth in her eyes.

"Pshaw," Ruan replied dismissively, though a jolt of pleasure traversed him at her words, and he struggled to keep a grin from erupting on his face. What was wrong with him? He was a Duke, he wasn't supposed to wag his tail like a puppy when a woman declared him adorable!

"We have embarrassed His Grace," Olive whispered to Mrs Hogg, linking her arm through the older woman's. The two ladies headed in the direction of the Blue Parlour, with Ruan following behind. Tea was served in the bright, airy room, which looked out over the rose garden. Mrs Hogg bustled about, directing skittish maids, and not sitting down herself until Olive begged her to.

"Tell me more about Pemberton Hall," she pleaded, and with a show of humble reluctance -which soon passed -Mrs Hogg took a seat on the divan opposite Olive, and began to school her on the running of the house. It was all new information to Ruan, who had not known how much effort went in to keeping a home he rarely frequented running smoothly. Cleaning, gardening, repair work — it amazed him what went on in the house without his knowledge.

"It sounds like you are doing a most admirable job, Mrs Hogg," Olive said with a smile, as the housekeeper finished speaking. Olive turned to Ruan, her eyebrows raised, "Does it not, your Grace?"

"Lud," Ruan gave his housekeeper a roguish smile, "I had no idea how much work you did. Remind me to give you a pay rise Mrs Hogg."

The older woman beamed with delight at the praise, and rose from her seat, brushing down her apron.

"Thank you, your Grace," she said with a neat bob of her knees, "Now I really must get back to work. I'll leave you to show Olive the rest of the house."

The door closed behind her with a firm click, leaving the Duke and his wife alone. A moment's silence ensued, in which Ruan stared fixedly at the China cup in his hand. It was absurdly small, and looked even smaller as his hands were so large, though the one in Olive's hand seemed a perfect fit. She was perfect; small and delicate, and utterly untouchable.

"Who is that?"

Ruan raised his eyes to where Olive was pointing, even though he knew instinctively what it was that had aroused her curiosity.

"That's Catherine," he said, standing up and walking over to the portrait which hung above the fire-place. The Blue Parlour had always been Catherine's favourite room in the house, so it had felt more appropriate to hang her picture here. He started slightly, as he felt a touch on his sleeve, but relaxed when he realised it was Olive, who had come to stand beside him. She patted his hand consolingly as she gazed up at the picture of Catherine.

"She was very beautiful," she offered; for it was the truth. Catherine had always been a beauty, with dark locks and deep brown eyes set against alabaster pale skin. It was a restless beauty however; even in the portrait she looked agitated, as though she wished to be anywhere than there.

"Polly told me everything," Olive said, after they had stood in reflective silence for a moment. Ruan turned to look at her in confusion; "Told you everything about what?"

"About Catherine. About you and Catherine. Don't be angry with Polly," she added quickly, seeing the look on Ruan's face. "She just wanted me to know what a kind and generous hearted man you are. And you are, Ruan, you truly are."

Her soft voice speaking his name caused him to shiver with desire, and her hand on his seemed to burn his very skin. He encircled her wrist with his own hand, and pulled her gently toward him, so that she was pressed against his chest.

"If you think that, my dear," he whispered, looking down into her green eyes, "Then will you consent to be my wife?"

Olive licked her lips, a nervous act, no doubt, but one which left Ruan aching with need for her.

"Perhaps," she consented, shyly dropping her eyes to his chest, "Though we did agree that a courtship is not complete until the couple have danced together at least once, did we not?"

Ruan groaned at her teasing words; he was aching for her so much that it was nearly painful. Still, at least she seemed to have softened toward him; in fact, he would go so far as to say that she now actually appeared to like him. A marked improvement on the first days of their marriage.

"I wish," he said softly, and she glanced up at him again, her eyes full of questions. "I wish that I had courted you properly the first time Olive," he continued, feeling relief as he divested himself of the guilt he felt. "I'm sorry, I'm so sorry that I went about everything the wrong way." He watched his wife frown as she considered his apology.

"I wish you had too, your Grace," she finally replied in a light, teasing tone. "Now the future of our marriage rests on your ability to Waltz..." It would be the best waltz of her life, Ruan thought with determination. Then once it was done, he would take her by the hand and lead her to the nearest bedroom - scandal be damned!

"Gemini, you look beautiful!"
Poppy and Alexandra both danced around Olive as she descended the
stairs of the boarding house. Their enthusiasm was infectious, and Olive
reluctantly had to admit that the dress that Jane had loaned her, was
most becoming. It was a dark, emerald green, which suited her
colouring perfectly. The empire line dress flared beneath the bust into a
light, frothy skirt of silk. She had initially protested to Polly that it was
too small around the bust, for Jane had a far slighter frame than she,
but the Northern woman had given a ribald laugh at the suggestion that
it looked improper.
"Sure isn't that what every woman wants?" Polly had laughed, "A dress
that emphasises rather than restricts one's assets?"
Polly had flushed then, and murmured an apology; their relationship had
recovered from the initial lies they had both told each other at the start
of it. Though Polly now regularly faltered when she addressed her, not
knowing whether to call Olive by her name, or address her as "Your
Grace".
"You both look beautiful as well," Olive offered the twins, for they were a
sight to behold. They were dressed in identical gowns of soft lilac, their
blonde curls tied high on their heads —it was almost impossible to tell
them apart. A fact not lost on their Aunt, who frowned as she exited the
drawing room and saw their attire.
"No funny business," she said, wagging a finger at the pair when she
saw them, and in response the twins tried to look wide-eyed and
innocent. "I will not have a repeat of what happened at Lady Amberley's
ball."
"What happened at Lady Amberley's ball?" Olive asked, her interest
piqued.
"Oh a ghastly, ancient, decrepit, old man thought to court me," Poppy
scowled at the memory.
"So the twins decided to play a trick on the poor soul," her Aunt
interrupted, a frown on her face. She would not encourage their hi-jinx,
despite how infectious their exuberance was.
"We didn't tell Sir Boras that there were two of us," Alexandra
continued, "And so he got an awful fright when one of us exited one
door, only to appear a few seconds later on the other side of the
ballroom."
"And when he danced with Poppy, I kept popping up at the side of the
ballroom and waving at him. He thought he was having an apoplectic
fit!"
"He nearly did have a fit," Augusta admonished and cast Olive a
pleading look; "I pray my dear, that you'll keep an eye on these two and
keep them out of mischief."

"I'll try," Olive promised the older woman, though secretly she doubted anyone's ability to keep the twins from doing what they wanted. The only other lady that had decided to accompany them to the ball was Petronella Devoy, who was resplendent in a gown of dark red, which complimented her dark, lustrous locks perfectly. Olive had almost forgotten that Petronella was the daughter of a Viscount, but the exquisite material of her dress, coupled with the diamonds around her neck, promptly reminded her.

There was no carriage to take them to Jarvis House, so the women walked, arms linked, in high spirits. The sun was beginning to set, and the sea at the bottom of the steep hill was deep purple, streaked with flashes of orange and gold. The house was all lit up, and as they hurried up the sweeping driveway they could hear the sounds of voices and music coming from within.

Jane stood at the door to greet them. She wore a very becoming gown of taupe and her hair was dressed high on her head.

"Oh wonderful, I was hoping that was you," she once the ladies had reached the front door. Her glasses were absent, and she squinted at each member of the entourage, trying to discern who was who.

"Where are your spectacles Jane?" Poppy queried, as their hostess blindly led them through the entrance hall, to the ballroom.

"Oh, Julian says they're too hideous to wear to a ball," Jane said plainly, "And that the guests would run off if they caught sight of me in them."

"What nonsense," Poppy frowned, her face a picture of the annoyance the Liv felt. Lord Deveraux was seriously beginning to grate on her nerves.

"Yes, you're beautiful with your glasses," Alexandra interjected, "They magnify your eyes, so that it's like looking at some mythical nymph when one is speaking with you!"

Jane flushed, and laughed at Alexandra's statement, though she did look rather pleased.

"I'm afraid it's just a small affair," she confided, as she led the ladies into the magnificent ballroom. "Nothing like the parties one attends in London."

As Olive took in the scene before her, she felt she had to disagree. The ballroom of Jarvis House was huge, with double height ceilings and chandeliers shedding twinkling light on the guests below. There was at least a hundred people present, many that Liv did not recognise, though one did catch her eye - Lord Keyford, who stood some distance from the crowd, surveying all the guests with dislike. She shivered, hoping that he would not spot her, not after their nasty encounter in the inn. Luckily her view of him was blocked by a rather large man who stepped into her path.

"Ruan," she said happily, as her husband gave a low, courteous bow.

"My lady," his eyes twinkled as he stood, "Might I request the pleasure of the first waltz?"

"You may."

She beamed up at him, as giddy as a school-girl, unaware that Jane still stood close by.

"The waltz is the last dance of the night, your Grace," Jane quipped, "So you'll have to dance with a few other ladies, before you get to Olive." Olive could see the frustration on her husband's face, and it amused her no end. It was secretly thrilling to have such a powerful, masculine man ready to do her bidding.

"Oh, yes Jane," she nodded, hiding her smile behind her hand. "His Grace must dance with the twins, Miss Devoy, you, and some of the ladies from the village. It's only right."

"Oh is it?"

Ruan cocked an eyebrow, an amused smile playing on his sinfully beautiful lips. Olive felt her mouth go dry as their eyes locked; his smoldering gaze promised retribution, and her stomach fluttered at the thought of what he might do. She recalled their brief, passionate embrace aboard The Elizabeth, and instantly regretted her plan to loan the Duke out to her friends. She wanted to be in his arms, she wanted to feel his heartbeat in his chest, she wanted to—

"Olive?"

Jane peered at her curiously, despite her shortsightedness she could tell that Olive was distracted and flustered. "Are you alright?"

"Just a trifle hot, Jane," she responded, fanning her hand against her flaming cheeks, "Perhaps we shall fetch a glass of ratafia?"

The two friends linked arms and went in search of refreshments, though as they walked Olive could feel the burning gaze of her husband on her back. Something had changed between the two of them; she now craved his company and his touch. She wanted to see that amused smile spread across his handsome face when she teased him, she wanted to hear his dry laughter at her jokes. If she didn't know any better, Olive would think she was falling in love with her own husband...

"Things are going well, between you and His Grace," Jane whispered, once they were out of earshot. It was not a question but a statement; apparently Olive's feelings for the Duke were plain to see.

"I think that you were right," Olive whispered back, stealing a glance at her handsome husband, who was asking one of the twins to dance. "He is a good man."

Their conversation was interrupted by the handsome Lord Payne, who, despite best efforts, looked rumpled and boyish in his dress coat and trousers.

"I say, Jane," he called happily, "I've been looking for you all over. If I didn't know any better, I'd think you were hiding from me!"

From the look on Jane's face, Olive guessed that this was exactly what her friend had been doing. Though, of course, the roguishly handsome Lord Payne would never dream that any lady would shun his company. Olive stifled a giggle as Jane desperately tried to squirm her way out of dancing with the dashing Duke-to-be, but her pleading fell on deaf ears, and she was led, blindly, to the floor for a boisterous quadrille.

"Your friend looks rather discomfited."

Olive turned to find Lord Somerset at her side, his handsome face turned toward the dance floor, where poor Jane was stumbling through the steps of the dance.

"Your friend ordered his sister to forgo her spectacles for the night," Olive replied archly in Jane's defence.

"Julian always was a prig," Lavelle muttered under his breath. Olive cast him a sidelong look; the Viscount seemed to be swaying on his feet. He was in his cups!

"What say you to a twirl around the floor?" Lavelle suggested, oblivious to Olive's look of alarm. She could not dance with a man so inebriated, it would surely end in disaster.However, before she could voice an excuse, Lavelle grabbed her by the hand, and led her to the centre of the floor.

"I hear you are to resume your post as Duchess," Lavelle commented, as Olive took his hand to dance down the line of guests. They took their places opposite each other, and because of the distance between them Olive could not reply.

"Good old Everleigh," Lavelle continued, as after a few bars they met again to join hands and twirl. "He always got the women to fall for him." Olive glanced at the Viscount in confusion; from the way he was speaking it seemed as though he didn't like Ruan —though the two had been friends for years. She remained silent for the rest of the dance and hastily excused herself once it had ended. As the next set started, she hid herself behind a large, marble column and peered out at the guests on the floor. It reminded her of the night in June, when she had hid at Lady Jersey's, but this time the dark, handsome man who had frightened her so, was the very person she wished to be with. She watched Ruan dancing with Poppy—or was it Alexandra?— with an ache in her heart. He was so striking; true, if one believed the rumours, he could be considered intimidating —but she knew the truth. The Duke of Ruin was possibly the most virtuous person in room.

As he twirled the twin in his arms, his eye caught Olive's and he gave a wink. She flushed, hoping no one had spotted, and stepped back further into the shadows.

"What's a pretty thing like you doing hiding in the dark?"

Olive whirled around to see who had spoken, her heart hammering in her chest. Standing in darkness, by the open French doors, was Lavelle, and he had a pistol aimed straight at her.

"Say a word and I'll shoot," he threatened - though he needn't have, for Olive was dumb with shock. The blonde haired Viscount grabbed her by the wrist and pulled her toward him, and the open door.

"W-what?" Olive at last found her voice, but it was silenced as Lavelle placed a gloved hand over her mouth.

"It's nothing personal Olive," he whispered harshly, as he pulled her out into the darkness of the garden, "It's just revenge."

Drat!

Ruan deposited Poppy—or was it Alexandra?—at the side of the ballroom once their dance had ended, and went in search of his wife, but she was no where to be seen. Ruan scanned the room, thanking his lucky stars that he was one of the tallest men there, but still he could not see her. He began to make his way toward the refreshment table, where he had spotted Jane, but his path was blocked by a rather familiar face.

"Lord Keyford," he said, pausing mid-step, as he came face to face with his father in law. The last time the two men had met, was five years ago at Catherine's funeral. The atmosphere had been tense, to say the least, and Ruan had left St. Jarvis convinced that his father in law wanted him dead —something he was still sure of now.

"You decided to return," Keyford said, his words slurred. It was obvious that the old man was drunk, even at a distance Ruan could smell the overpowering scent of alcohol on his breath.

"Aye," Ruan answered slowly, carefully watching the older man's reaction. "I thought it was about time I showed my face, even if it's the last face that some people might want to see."

The old man looked at him curiously and to Ruan's surprise his eyes became misty. "I hope you're not referring to me, lad," Keyford said, his voice thick with emotion. "For I know all that you did for Catherine, and you're forever welcome here, by me, at least."

"You know?" Ruan's face paled; what exactly did the old man know, and who had told him?

"Mrs Hogg." As though he had read his thoughts, Lord Keyford offered up the name of his informant. "I met her one day at Catherine's grave, and I'm ashamed to say that I began to abuse your reputation terribly — Mrs Hogg soon set me straight."

Ruan swallowed in lieu of a reply, he could not think of what to say in response to the man that his late wife had despised. Keyford seemed different now — defeated, almost as though his daughter's death had affected him profoundly.

"Catherine always attracted ne'er-do-wells; if it wasn't Lord Somerset breaking her heart, it was that Birmingham chap. I should have thanked you properly, when you took her under your care. You did her a great kindness Everleigh."

"Lavelle?" Ruan felt a stab of confusion, "What does Lavelle have to do with anything?"

"He proposed to Catherine, the last summer he was here," Keyford spat angrily, "Then disappeared to London and promptly forgot about her. Is it any wonder she ended up in the arms of that scoundrel Birmingham?"

Ruan felt as though he had been punched in the stomach; he had not known that Lavelle had proposed to Catherine. It was a despicable thing to have done, to have raised her hopes and then dashed them —but they had been young men.

"Perhaps there was some misunderstanding?"

"No misunderstanding," Keyford was firm, "And then he had the gall to accuse her of betrayal when she married you. I tell you, when I saw him in Southampton, not two weeks ago, I was tempted to run him over with my carriage."

Realisation dawned in Ruan's mind, slowly at first, but like a gas lamp catching flame he soon saw the light. It had been Lavelle all along; the attacks, the accidents, the attempts on his life, even the two roses at Catherine's grave. Lavelle had not arrived in Southampton to assist his friend —he had come to pay the man he had hired to kill him!

"Good God," he whispered, glancing frantically around the room to see where his nefarious friend was.

"Everything all right Everleigh?"

Ruan nodded curtly, and left Keyford standing in the middle of the ballroom, as he went in search of Lavelle.

"Have you seen Somerset?" he asked Jane urgently, once he had reached her side.

"I have seen no one, your Grace," the young woman replied miserably, "I can't see past the end of my nose without my spectacles. The waltz is soon though, I know that much. You'd best go fetch Olive before somebody steals her away!"

Although Jane's voice was light and teasing, her words sent a jolt of fear through Ruan. The last time he had spotted Olive, she had been hiding in a dark alcove. He made his way to where she had stood, when she had smiled at him, but there was no one there. The curtains on the French doors, which had been left open to catch a breeze, rustled slightly as they were stirred by a gust of wind. A dash of colour of the floor caught his eye, and he stooped down to inspect the item. It was a ribbon, a green ribbon: the same one which Olive had worn on her dress. It had caught his eye because he had vividly imagined untying the thing once he had her alone in his bedchamber.

Silently he exited the doors, which led to a dark veranda. He could see signs of a struggle —an overturned urn of flowers, a wrought-iron chair on its side, and most worryingly of all, a lone slipper. He hunkered down and picked it up; it was small, black and utterly anonymous, but he knew instinctively that it belonged to Olive.

Agitated he stood, and made to return to the ballroom, but a confused voice called out to him from the shadows.

"I say Everleigh, is that you?" It was Lord Deveraux, relaxing and smoking a cheroot. "Finished already?"

His old friend gave a rather saucy laugh, which left Ruan perplexed. "Finished what?"

"With your wife. I heard you dragging her away, old chap," Julian guffawed with amusement, before taking another drag on his cigar. "Well done, you finally convinced her."

Ruan near staggered at Julian's words —the stupid fool had heard his wife, who had obviously been putting up a fight, being dragged away into a dark garden, and he had done nothing!

"That wasn't me," he bit harshly, to a startled Lord Deveraux, "That was Lavelle. He wants revenge for Catherine and so he's taken my wife."

"W-what?"

Ruan had no time to explain to Julian what was happening, instead he barged through the ballroom, and up to his bedroom. He had never been filled with such rage; his pistol lay in the drawer of his bedside table, and never before had he felt so compelled to use it. If someone had told him a week before that he would want to put a bullet through his best friend's heart, he would have told them they were insane —now, at that moment, he would gladly have riddled Lavelle with as many bullets as he could shoot.

"I say," a voice called, as Ruan came barrelling down the stairs to the entrance hall, "What's all this about Somerset kidnapping your wife?"

It was Lord Payne, slightly breathless, but wearing a look of determination on his young face.

"He absconded with Olive about half an hour ago," Ruan snapped, not breaking his stride. The younger man jogged alongside him, his face worried.

"Any idea where he might have taken her?"

Ruan paused just outside the door, thinking.

"There's one road," he said, as he once again began to stride in the direction of the stables. "It goes in two directions."

"So, I go one way, you go the other."

Ruan glanced at Payne in surprise; the young man was known as a high-spirited rake, but now his tone was determined and Ruan was glad that he was there. Payne looked grim and angry, and Ruan knew that he would gladly do anything to protect Olive—even shoot Lavelle.

"You go in the direction of Truro," he said, "I'll go toward the cliffs, it leads back to Lavelle's home, he might have gone that way. Do you have a pistol?"

Payne patted the breast pocket of his dinner jacket. "Always."

He might have made a wry comment about a man with a predication for married women needing to carry one at all times, but this was not the moment. The Duke and the Duke-in-waiting, dashed across the front yard, to the side of the house where the stables were located. The grooms inside were still mucking out for the night, but jumped to attention when they caught sight of the pair. They saddled two horses for the men and within five minutes Ruan was away, galloping down the pebbled drive of Jarvis House. Once he reached the gates he went right, while Payne went left with a shout of encouragement. Ruan leaned low against his mount's neck, urging him on in a fast gallop. He hoped that Lavelle would be slowed down by Olive struggling, for he had a large lead on him.

Ruan galloped ferociously through the dark night, ignoring the town of St. Jarvis, which was lit up below him. The cliff path was in darkness, but luckily the night was clear and the three-quarter moon illuminated his way. Never before had he been struck by such fear; the thought of Olive afraid or in pain was like a sword through his chest. This feeling was new and utterly unfamiliar; he had not known that he had the capacity to care so much for another human being.

"Faster," he urged his steed, slapping the horse's flank with his crop. He didn't usually ride so hard, and his thighs screamed in protest at the strenuous exercise, but he ignored the pain.

Finally, horse and rider came to a sharp bend in the road. The path, if he chose to follow it, went further inland, but if he went left he would reach the edge of the rugged cliffs.

Ruan paused, to consider his options. As he did so he heard a sound from his left; it was hard to hear exactly what it was, over the crashing of the waves below, but instinctively he rode towards it. He directed his horse over the grass and heather, until they were nearly at the cliff edge —and then he saw them. Olive was struggling valiantly against Lavelle, who had his arm around her neck and was dragging her across to where the cliff ended abruptly.

"Olive!"

Her name was torn from his mouth, and it flew across the space between them on the harsh, unforgiving breeze. Lavelle paused and looked up; a manic grin spread across his face as he spotted Ruan.

"You're too late," he roared above the howling wind, "Say goodbye to your wife Everleigh."

Panic seized Ruan at his words, but Olive, brave, resourceful Olive, took advantage of Lavelle's distracted state, to deliver a sharp elbow to his stomach. The Viscount doubled over, winded, letting go of the grip he had on the Duchess. Pale-faced Olive stumbled away from him, running in the direction of Ruan, who was in turn barrelling toward her.

"You're safe," he whispered as he caught her in his arms. He swiftly pushed her behind him, to protect her from any harm and began advancing on Lavelle.

"Why?" he asked, as he withdrew his pistol from his breast pocket. "Why do this Henry?"

"You ruined everything," his friend snarled, reaching inside his own jacket and fumbling for his weapon. "You stole Catherine from me and then you killed her. You don't deserve happiness, you don't deserve to live."

"Ruan didn't kill Catherine," Olive was shaking her head, her eyes fixed on the pistol that Lavelle now gripped. "She killed herself —he kept it secret so that she could have a decent burial."

"Lies!" Wild-eyed Lavelle backed away from the Duke and Duchess, his pistol still pointed at Ruan.

"It's the truth," Ruan bit out, "She was afflicted with sadness —a sadness that you helped perpetuate when you abandoned her for a life of vice in London. Why do you think she wrote to me when she discovered she was pregnant by Birmingham? Because she knew I was her true friend—she knew I would return to her. But you, you'd already broken her heart Henry, you'd already treated her like dirt upon your shoe."

"It's not true," the Viscount shook his head, and took another step backward. "You killed her, you did, you did—"

"Henry, no."

Ruan watched in horror as his oldest friend took another step back and lost his footing on the loose, stony edge of the cliff. He seemed to stay suspended, mid-air, for one second, his eyes awash with confusion and fear. Ruan raced forward, but it was too late, by the time he reached the cliff edge, Lavelle was plummeting toward the rocks, some fifty feet below.

"Don't look," Ruan ordered Olive, who had come to stand by his side. He drew her toward him, pressing her face against his chest so she would not have to see the horrible sight below.

"Is he..?"

Ruan nodded, unable to speak as a tide of emotion seemed set to drown him. Lavelle had been his best friend since they were both three-foot high, but for the past five years the man had secretly hated him and wished him dead.

"Come," Ruan put his arms around Olive's shoulders, and guided her to where the two horses now stood, grazing on the flora of the sea-cliffs. "We need to get back to Somerset House and fetch some help retrieving Lavelle's body."

He also needed a stiff glass of brandy and few moments alone to reflect on what had happened. He helped Olive to mount Lavelle's steed, then jumped into the saddle of his own. The Duke and Duchess travelled back to Jarvis House in silence, each lost in their own thoughts.

"Oh, you're safe. Thank goodness."

Jane, once more bespectacled, stood on the steps of Jarvis House to greet them. Lord Payne, who was thoroughly dusty and covered in a sheen of sweat at her side.

"Where's Lavelle?" he called to Ruan, who was helping Olive to dismount. The Duke threw the younger man a look that spoke volumes, which Payne returned with a grim nod of understanding.

"The guests have all left," Jane said, ushering Olive and Ruan inside. She guided them to the drawing room, where she ordered a pot of tea be fetched for Olive and something stronger for the Duke.

"Does anyone know what happened?" Ruan asked urgently, his mind already working to see how they could salvage the situation.

"Just myself, Lord Payne and Julian," Jane offered, handing Olive a steaming cup of tea. "We weren't quite sure exactly what was happening, so we didn't tell the other guests."

"Good," Ruan relaxed, "Let's keep it that way. Lavelle is dead, he fell off the cliffs just by Fisherman's Cove. We will tell no one of what he did, for his family's sake— Julian can circulate a rumour that he was in his cups when he left."

"You're going to pretend it was a tragic accident?"

Olive spoke for the first time since they had arrived, her face a picture of confusion. Ruan nodded; he hated Lavelle for the danger he had put his wife in, but he did not want to ruin his family's name, for Lavelle had brothers who lived around the locale and it was they who would bear the brunt of his treachery.

"Good God man, you're far more noble than I," Lord Payne said, taking a large bite out of a sandwich and looking at Ruan with awe.

"He's the most noble man that I have ever met," Olive whispered proudly, taking Ruan's hand in her own and squeezing it tightly. Ruan felt a stirring of pleasure at her words. They were both nearly finished their drinks, and Olive looked as tired as he felt.

"Shall I take you home?" he suggested, thinking to leave her at the boarding house, as he had every other night.

"Yes," his wife held his gaze, "Take me back to Pemberton Hall, Ruan. I'm ready to go home."

Liv could feel her husband's heart beating in his chest as she rested against it. He cradled her with one arm, his other hands gently holding the reins of the horse that was bringing them back to Pemberton Hall. No words had passed between man and wife once they had left Jarvis House. Instead Ruan had lifted her, as though she weighed nothing, into the saddle of his horse, before hopping up behind her. The journey was both pleasant and arduous. It felt wonderful to be held in the arms of a man as strong as the Duke, but the butterflies in her stomach had erupted at his closeness, so that she felt almost sick with excitement. Pemberton Hall lay in darkness when they arrived, Ruan guided the horse to the stables, banging on the door to rouse one of the grooms.

"Oh, Ruan, don't," Olive protested, "I can wait here while you tend to the horse, don't wake the poor men."

"My dear," her husband took her by the waist and pulled her toward him. "You may be able to wait, but I cannot."

A bleary eyed young groom opened the door to the living quarters of the stables, interrupting their embrace.

"Sorry to disturb your sleep Keats," her husband gave the lad an apologetic smile, "But I need you to stable him. I'm in rather a rush."

Olive felt her face flame with embarrassment as her husband took her by the hand and led her across the cobbled yard toward the back entrance of the house. They entered Pemberton Hall through the kitchen door, Ruan leading her commandingly up the servant's stairs, to the third floor.

"Oh," he paused when they reached the hallway, a look of dismay on his face. "I suppose that wasn't a very glamorous way to bring a Duchess into her new home."

He looked genuinely crestfallen and Olive had to stifle a laugh, such was his dismay.

"The hallway rather makes up for the lack of decor on the way up," Olive offered, for it did. The arched ceilings were covered in frescoes, and the wallpaper was heavily embossed. A thick Persian carpet ran the length of the hall, inviting the walker in the direction of an impressive set of double doors, that Olive knew would lead to the Duke's suites.

"If you're impressed by the hallway, then you'll faint at the sight of the bedroom," Ruan growled, lifting her up in his arms and carrying her toward his room. "Though dear God please don't faint. I've had the ignominious pleasure of being, possibly, the only Duke of Everleigh to have two marriages go unconsummated for any length of time."

Olive bit back a giggle at his self-deprecating words. She felt snug in his arms and was grateful for their support, for her knees felt weak with nerves and anticipation. Ruan near kicked the door open, in his haste to get inside. He placed Olive gently on the bed, then began to tear at the cravat around his neck and the buttons on his shirt.

Olive watched him from beneath her lashes, feeling suddenly shy. Her husband lifted his shirt above his head to reveal a toned, muscular stomach like a washboard and a chest that was thick with dark curls. She sat up and hesitantly reached a hand out to touch his chest. The skin on skin contact made her husband pause, and he placed his hand over hers, just above his heart. "I love you," he said simply, pressing her hand close to his flesh so that she could hear his heartbeat.

"And I you," Olive whispered, for the love she felt for him had pierced through her on the cliffs, when she thought that Lavelle would shoot him. She had never felt so strongly for anyone, as she did for the Duke, and the thought made her a little nervous. Her feelings were obviously displayed on her face, for Ruan stroked her cheek softly; "Are you certain that you're ready?"

Despite the passion which burned in his eyes, Olive knew that if she told her husband that she was not ready yet, that he would stop. The only thing was, she didn't want him to. As she nodded her head, he dropped his lips to hers and kissed her gently. The soft feel of his skin, contrasting the hardness of the muscles beneath, left her dizzy and light headed. With assured hands her husband began to undress her, working the buttons of her dress as though he was a trained ladies maid and not a Duke.

"You're rather adept at that," Olive commented, feigning humour to hide her nerves.

"There's a lot of things I'm very good at," her husband replied, his mouth quirking with amusement. His hands lifted her dress over her head, and soon she was lying naked beneath him. Any fear or trepidation that she might have felt, was soon swept away on a tide of pleasure. Her husband was a skilled love-maker, and though at first it hurt slightly, soon she became used to the feel of him. Within minutes she was breathless, as waves of pleasure—that she had not known were possible—washed over her. Sensing that she was spent the Duke finished with a low groan, collapsing on top of her and cradling her in his arms.

"That was rather good," she whispered to him across the pillow, when a few minutes of breathless silence had passed. She could not believe that the beautiful man lying next to her was her husband, and that she would wake up the next morning —and every morning— to the wondrous sight of him.

"Rather good?" Ruan huffed, evidently displeased with her choice of words. "I obviously wasn't doing my job properly if it was only rather good."

"It can get better?" Olive glanced at him innocently, knowing that he would rise to the bait of her teasing.

"A hundred times better," Ruan said, his face filled with need as he pinned her beneath his strong forearms. "I'm afraid you'll have to get used to this Olive."

"Used to what?" she asked, reaching up with her hand and smoothing the lock of hair that had fallen into his eyes.

"To being in my bed," her husband replied, with a smile that could only be described as pure wicked. "For I won't be letting you leave it for quite some time."

ABOUT THE AUTHOR

Claudia Stone was born in South Africa but moved to Plymouth as a young girl. Having trained as an actress at RADA, she moved to New York to pursue her dream of acting on Broadway in 1988. She never did see her name in lights, but she did meet a wonderful Irishman called Conal who whisked her away to the wilds of Kerry, where she has lived ever since.

Claudia and Conal have three children, a dairy farm and a St. Bernard called Bob. When she has any time left over, Claudia enjoys reading Regency as well as writing it.

If you would like to contact Claudia, you can connect with her on Goodreads or email claudiastoneauthor@mail.com

Printed in Poland
by Amazon Fulfillment
Poland Sp. z o.o., Wrocław

49284736R00066